The Ten Million Mile Man

The Ten Million Mile Man

Bob LaPlante

Rutledge Books, Inc.   Danbury, CT

Rutledge Books, Inc.
107 Mill Plain Road, Danbury, CT 06811
1-800-278-8533

Manufactured in the United States of America

Cataloging in Publication Data
LaPlante, Robert J.
The ten million mile man

ISBN: 1-58244-026-3

1. Diplomatic couriers -- United States -- Biography.
2. LaPlante, Bob.
920

Dedication

For my Navigator, Buddy and Ally, my son Erik.

As life is action and passion, it is required of a man that he should share the passion and action of his time, at peril of being judged not to have lived.

— Oliver Wendell Holmes, Jr.

Introduction

Growing up in the vast bastion of America's Great Lakes, I started to "collect" distant lands to mount in my postage stamp album. The exotic scenes on these colorful little squares were impressive and caused me to wonder what splendors awaited the rays of our setting sun. How would a boy like me ever reach those fabled shores and actually tread their sands and hear the babble of such impossibly faraway places?

World War II swirled over our lives like an arctic blizzard and my country collection began in earnest. However, the smashed islands and cities of the South Pacific and the Orient were rubble tragedies, and it was not until later that I would see the classic centers of the postwar world.

Then that miracle of midcentury, the GI Bill of Rights, flung open the gates of higher education so that I could join the millions who switched from uniforms to universities. My yearning for the overseas world did not subside during my University of Michigan days, but one startling day I discovered the existence of a small coterie of professional travelers, the Corps of U.S. Diplomatic Couriers. They were attached to the U.S. Foreign Service and Department of State, with a singular mission: carry, safeguard and deliver America's foremost secrets by diplomatic pouch to over 100 U.S. embassies and consulates around the globe. After several years of applying and waiting, I was appointed to the Corps of Diplomatic Couriers in 1950. Now, four decades and more than 10,000,000 miles later, I have crisscrossed the earth and filled my stamp albums and my mind with vivid scenes drawn from the darkest corners of our planet. Studying my 25 years of notes written en route, I concluded that this record should share its excitement of a unique life-adventure by one of history's most-traveled men.

Here you will meet such giants of this century as Doctor Albert Schweitzer in Central Africa, President Harry S. Truman in Washington, D.C., Ernest Hemingway in Italy, Maestro Duke Ellington in Germany, and Rear Admiral Richard Byrd in New Zealand. This is a journey equal to 40 trips to the Moon; fasten your seat belts!

BL
Fitzgerald-Forest
May, 1999

With Hemingway in Venice

My gondola chopped across the Grand Canal of Venice to the dock at San Marco. Minutes before landing I noticed another gondola heading for the same dock; it carried one passenger, a big man who seemed at a distance to be silvery white from his neck to the top of his head. I was busy with my camera and took no further notice of this converging craft. I paid off my gondolier and started up the gangplank. In a few strides I was at the second gondola's mooring point precisely as it touched the dock. As an old navy man, I instinctively steadied the bow for the boatman and was surprised to hear his passenger shout something to me in English, "Where are the other people?" I looked around to confront my questioner. He was Ernest Hemingway, and I was his one-man literary general—the least likely person to meet the great writer and the best prepared to relish it.

His closely-cropped white hair ran from his neck to the top of his head like the mane of a proud lion. As Hemingway stepped ashore, I fell into stride with him and explained that I was traveling alone but had chosen San Marco's plaza and Harry's Bar as my starting points for a Venetian sojourn. He shouted to the gondolier to wait for him and then led the way to Harry's Bar. Suddenly he stopped, slowed me down with his arm, and leaned down to push open the door to Harry's which is located below the sidewalk level. He motioned me through the door and I stepped down into the midmorning warmth and winey air of the renowned Italian bar.

The bar was crowded. It was March and customers still preferred the cozy interior to the cool, rain-splashed outdoor tables. EH strode across the room and waved me over to meet Mary Hemingway who was sitting at a table which was distinguished by several plates of small, triangular sandwiches which were set out. We were settling into chairs as a dozen people filed down through the entrance and converged at the Hemingway table. Each had a copy of a Hemingway book translated into Italian, just purchased from a bookstore. Mary explained that these were their shipmates from the steamship *Africa* which had just brought them from Mombasa to Venice. The author autographed each book with enthusiasm and personal remarks for his departing shipmates as I studied him: thick arms with recent scars, solid frame, intense, agile writing pose.

Morning Sours

The book-clutchers with their autographs dispersed quickly, and a bright tray of whiskey sours materialized without order. Good fare for outstanding company and conversation, the sours and sandwiches. I did not have a Hemingway volume with me, but perhaps he would autograph my thick, old diplomatic passport which bulged like a book with its dozens of extension pages and countless visas. He entered his signature and added an OK. Mary added hers and began a careful examination of the million miles of diplomatic courier travel which were stamped by visas through the pages. I showed them the entry point on the Finnish-Russian border where I learned that Ernest Hemingway had been killed in an African air crash. He smiled broadly at his reference and as I quoted him saying after his rescue, "My luck, she is still good."

I was intrigued to be sharing drinks, sandwiches and conversation with the man who put so many books on my grandfather's shelves. Reared in the Upper Peninsula of Michigan, the locales of early Hemingway stories, I had local insight that interested the writer. In a beautiful tale of trout versus youth, he placed the Big Two-Hearted

River at a hamlet called Seney. Seney was a logging site well-known to our family, and when I asked the author why he ignored the real name of the local river, the Fox, he sharply reminded me that the Big Two-Hearted was poetry, better story stuff, and that is why he had moved it a couple of dozen miles to the Southwest. So it is that the power of the pen can move nations . . . and rivers too. He did not seem amused when I maintained my preference for the Fox.

I told him of the big browns and rainbows I had caught in my hometown Thompson Creek, and his eyes and tone of voice assured Mary and me that Hemingway was into one of his prime subjects. Wyoming, Idaho, the Caribbean and Peru rolled off his recollections of great fishing moments, but the Upper Penisula, "the UP," had been one of his first fishing objectives. He had read Stewart Edward White's tales of the big timbering days in the UP and sensed in them the raw, wild flavor of the vast tract of land that lay across the Straits of Mackinac.

I asked about his hand and arm scars and he launched into an enthusiastic report of a bushfire he had fought in Kenya as an honorary game warden, this after the two airplane crashes that had tried to take him "out of the fight twice in a couple of days." EH spoke lightly and precisely, with a very clear *t* in the word writing. He thoroughly loved the barroom-parliament, and was relaxed and at the same time, intense. Listening carefully, he leaned forward and addressed Mary and me, one at a time. He had lost some left eyesight and had kidney and intestinal troubles from the crashes . . . spent most of the cruise from Mombasa to Italy in his bunk. He had a heavy forehead scar and brown bloodshot eyes. He wore a wool jacket, sweater, tie, cap, loafers; she was trim, in an informal suit, low shoes.

Shot Before Breakfast

Senator McCarthy and his two investigators, Cohn and Schine, were prominent names in the news then. Hemingway saw a menace to U.S. freedoms in the political antics of these gentlemen. They should be invited to a country where dueling is legal and shot before breakfast. EH flexed his shooting hand and said it wasn't healed enough to do the job. If the injuries did not heal and he could not write, he might have to turn to positive work.

Several hours passed in this pleasant and distinguished company; there were no intrusions at our table, just the dutiful visitations of the waiter. EH called for the check and waved off my attempt to contribute. He signed the bill; must have a running account with Harry's.

The Hemingways were going to lunch at Vista Buona and invited me to join them, but yours truly was so underwhelmed by this unique encounter with his literary hero that he declined, citing a tight schedule of trains to the tiny lands of Europe which we did not see on diplomatic courier runs: San Marino, Liechtenstein, Monaco, and Andorra. I have regretted this decision every day for half my life. EH picked up my heavy passport and thumbed through the many pages to the place where he and Mary had signed their names, entered "Vista Buona," and told me if I changed my mind, to come to this place for lunch. In the Venetian manner, Hemingway had "held" his gondola.

As I walked them to the San Marco landing, I asked if I might take their picture. Mary liked the idea, "Papa, we never had a picture of us in a gondola." At last I heard the "Papa" used by family and close friends. Handshakes all around as I thanked them for the sours and sandwiches and the luncheon invitation. Yes, I would see that their gondola picture went to their Cuban home. Since I was Paris-based, EH leaned forward with a message to Harry and Andy MacElhone of Harry's Bar in Paris: He was recuperating from the crashes and the bushfire in East Africa and would be back to see them.

Near-Riot in Cuba

They were two happy passengers as the gondola veered away to the mainstream of the Grand Canal. As I poked along the cobbled street to Piazza San Marco, I decided Hemingway had a midwestern U.S. accent with just a trace of the U.S. east. The gondola picture, which I prize, was copied and delivered to the Hemingways at their Fincá Vigia residence in Cuba but not without passing through a near-riot there. My aunt, who carried the picture, had arrived on the day Hemingway had been awarded the Nobel Prize for Literature, and the crush of cars and people, media representatives and traffic police engulfed the Fincá. Mary and a maid rescued my persevering aunt, served tea, and assured her that it was not always so riotous at their home. EH then appeared in the dining room with the gondola picture in his hand and asked my relative to express thanks to the diplomatic courier who took the picture in Venice.

A few short years later a courier colleague crossed my route in Brazil and handed me a fistful of personal mail. One envelope contained two cards. The first was black-bordered and bore only these three numbers: 5 5 5.

The second card bore Mary's paralyzing note: "Bob: Present this card for admittance to the funeral." Hemingway dead? This is how I learned that he had terminated his life in an ultimate resolution of that recurring theme of control-of-life-and-death that echoes through his works. Hemingway's own life of high adventure was his greatest story, a tale that unwound in far, dangerous corners of the earth. It led at last to a quiet country cemetery under the fir trees in the mountains of Idaho.

Close Call in Manila

The Manila night air was heavy with aromas as I left the wondrous Filipino eatery Bamboo Cloud where I had dined on exotic seafoods. I had waited until a soft evening rain fizzled out before starting the familiar walk to my nearby apartment. Over on the curve of Manila Bay a copra processing plant had perfumed the air with the agreeable odor of warm coconut meat, made all the more fragrant by the humidity of this tropical locale. It never occurred to me that this occasional evening walk might be dangerous, but I had a lot to learn.

As I passed the cafes and bars, bright music poured from them and I recognized "Ampola" and "You Belong to My Heart," far and away the most popular tunes of 1950s Manila. I didn't stop in for a nightcap on this occasion but just ambled along homeward bound.

The streets became silent as I left the bars behind me, and as I strolled, I began to hear the soft "pat-pat" of feet on the wet sidewalk. Someone was walking behind me, but I could not make out any identifying details in the dark. I moved ahead and paused just beyond a corner street lamp which quickly shone down on a short mountain tribesman who had apparently come down to the big city. He was shoeless and wearing short trousers and a straw hat. Over his shoulder was a dark, wet bag. I registered the scene and resumed my ramble, accompanied by the "pat-pat" of the hillman's feet. I routinely cut across the street. So did he. I then recrossed the street and picked up the pace of my stroll. So did he! "OK," said I, "this hunter is tracking me." My familiarity with this district told me that numerous residences and apartment houses posted guards at their entrances. I steered for a well-illuminated, stately residence as I pointed to my incessant tracker who was still bearing down on me. The two Filipino guards said nothing but pounced like panthers on the little tribesman. They seated him, and I was greatly impressed with his calm. The guards sized him up and reported that he was "stoned" on a narcotic nut he was chewing. This was a somewhat usual practice among the mountain people. They assured me I had not been in danger, and I was inclined to accept that scenario.

Before I could continue on my way home, I asked the guards to empty the sinister wet bag our visitor had slung over his shoulder. He clung to the sack and tried to run away. When he was returned forcibly and reseated, the bag was emptied onto a table. Twenty assorted pieces of jewelry and watches tumbled across the veneer. One larger item would not fall out. It was removed by hand. It was a heavy, very shiny machete, the axe of the Orient!

Secret Ransom

It was a rainy autumn in Madrid, a city that does not see much moisture in general. The Spanish diners, who flock to the open-air cafes, were driven inside by the wet weather, but this did not cause them to take their meals any earlier. The leisurely late dinner is traditional, and that suited me well. It was nearing midnight before I could find a table at Casa El Boti`n, my special destination. Several months earlier I had had the extraordinary pleasure of hearing the glories of Casa El Boti`n from a man who knew his bars and restaurants, Ernest Hemingway. It was in another Mediterranean city, Venice, that I sat with the great writer and his wife Mary and heard his recollections of Civil War Madrid, the renowned Prado Art Museum and of course an excellent restaurant, Casa El Boti`n. His morning routine was to write at a sunlit café table on the cobblestones of Plaza Mayor. At the sign of midday hunger, he would stride the few hundred yards to Boti`n and sit at a table close to the huge charcoal grilling racks, almost in the kitchen.

I conjectured that my chances of finding a Hemingway-type table were better if I dined late in the evening. When I entered, the maitre d', however, led me straight to a central table and, in view of the surprising number of guests, I could not object. The air was rich with wine sauces and grilled meats, and the aroma competed with the absolutely dazzling array of asparagus, endive, duck, salmon and strawberries. It was gastronomic Madrid at its best.

I had slowly eaten the tray of provincial asparagus and was enjoying a goblet of world-class Valdepenas when I became aware of a very happy foursome at an adjoining table. They were Americans, a gentleman, two ladies, and a teenage girl; and I decided that the distinguished vino had elevated their spirits, judging from the laughter and antics that enveloped them. When the wineglasses lost their red glow, the man arose, draped a napkin over his arm and waltzed around the chairs, refilling everyone's glass. Before returning to his seat, he ambled over to my table and scooped me out of my chair and plunked me down at his celebration table. I tried to explain that roast duck with wild rice would arrive at my table any minute, but the happy gang demanded that I remain with them. My waiter smiled and served a superb meal at my new location. I learned that Mel and Beatrice had flown off to Spain with their daughter and cousin from Texas where they had oil interests. Conversation and laughter rolled on, and the persistent Spanish diners slowly departed the comfortable precincts of Boti`n. Then the windows began to sparkle with a new shower, and the doorman announced that taxis would be difficult to find for an hour. Our jolly throng was certainly not in a hurry, so we had more wine, brandy, and cigars.

At that late hour the proprietor of Casa El Boti`n visited, first, the only other guests still remaining, and then our fivesome. In view of the unusual rain and the taxi delays, would we join him at his kitchen table as his guests. . .? Of course we all filed into the world's most sumptuous kitchen, if one could call it that. Massive dark wooden beams contrasted with gleaming copper shields all around and an array of huge glowing grill racks. Seven-foot wrought iron candleholders stood at attention around a large dining table where we were soon packed in like one happy family. Still more classic vinos were uncorked, and the ladies were served a bonus portion of ice cream and raspberries. It was the most enjoyable rain delay we could have imagined.

In that very relaxed, optimistic setting, I learned a chilling secret about my American tablemates. They were in nonstop ecstasy for a single dreadful reason, Beatrice told me. Their only child, this pretty teenager, had been kidnapped, held in a mountain cave for two days, and released unharmed when Mel made a dangerous but totally secret payment of an enormous ransom. He and Beatrice had made the decision to pay the ransom and not alert law authorities. They were convinced that they had secured their daughter's freedom by this direct action, irrespective of the "awful" ransom.

Kidnapping was a totally foreign subject to me. I asked, "How awful?"

"In excess of a million dollars," she replied. "Now you will forgive our craziness . . . this night, this happiness will never end for us . . . we will find a new home, another lifestyle . . . the return of our child has given us new lives."

A Cloud of Metal

Once you've adventured in a camping van, a mere automobile seems like a metal box. My young son and I covered much of Europe in our van, and we quickly came under the charm of roaming the Continent on the wheels of a complete personal environment. If we had music practice, schoolwork or reading to do, we did it on the spot wherever we were, in the Alps, on the Baltic shore, or in the Black Forest. We fished often and our fresh trout flew from stream to our van's frying pan in no time. We chilled juices and brews and wines in our refrigerator and entertained other travelers and fisherfolk in the mountains and along the waterways of Europe. Our self-contained music library was world-class, from Springsteen to Schubert to Slam Stewart. Foam rubber beds slept four adventurers and a foldaway desk with portable typewriter let me catch up on paperwork en route.

November had put a crimp in our warm weather wanderings, so we drove over to the boot shop in the U.S. Army's military store in Frankfurt am Main, Germany. We parked the venerable van and walked along a line of other vehicles to the shop. We were seated, examining boots, when a tremendous WHAM hit our ears; in the same instant a heavy, warm wave of air rushed over us. The lights flashed off and on, and the walls flapped like flags in the wind.

I leapt to the emergency door, which flew open to reveal a crowd of screaming people running away from a cloud of blue smoke and metal that began to rain loudly on the pavement. As soon as my son and I could hurtle down the emergency stairs, we ran toward our beloved van which seemed to be close to the center of this devastation. Military police slung a rope across the roadway and held everyone back from the site of the explosion. We edged as close as possible to our parking spot, looking for the van. Then we stared at each other: Gone. Empty. It had vanished. An ugly hole and torn metal were all that remained. Also missing was the line of other parked vehicles that had suddenly gone airborne.

"Terrorist bomb" filtered through the crowd's mutterings. This was faction-packed Frankfurt/M where bombings and other lethal incidents were common. The train of events unfolded: a medium-size sedan was packed with explosives, parked at the military store, and wired to a time fuse. When we parked and walked to the boot shop, we brushed right past this ticking time-bomb that exploded with terrifying power just 12 minutes later. Some eight vehicles were obliterated, and 52 people were injured, none fatally.

A young lady who was injured when a wall fell on her told me that one year later she continued to take oil baths to remove tiny glass fragments that had sprayed her skin.

The blue metallic smoke I had seen falling to earth was in fact part of our van, pulverized and air blasted by the powerful explosives. A van is just a personal environment on wheels, but as we walked home, alternately holding and examining the only thing we had left from our old buddy, a dead key, we saw in a flash that 12 minutes was all that separated us from Van Heaven.

A Diplomatic Courier Becomes a Diplomatic Bag

I had worked courier routes all over this earth and had navigated my pouches through many exotic seaports, mountain borders, and air terminals. And, of course, I had been called many names by people along the way. For example: His Excellency's Messenger (New Zealand), The President's Courier (East Africa), Le Courrier Diplomatique (Paris).

One fiercely hot day I found myself in Riyadh, Saudi Arabia, en route to San'a, Yemen. Checking over my documents for this run, I did a standing flip when I saw the name on my flight tickets: MR. DIPLOMATIC BAG. When you've been identified with diplomatic bags for four decades, you end up being called one!

How I Lost My Bus Seat "Down Under"

"Down Under" is Australia and almost everyone is called "mate." You hear the friendly term in every nook and cranny of Aussie life, and I like it—direct and informal! On a long bus ride down the Tasman Sea coast, I had stood for quite some time in the crowded vehicle before I sagged at last into an open seat. I was slowly adjusting to the luxury of being seated when an outrageously pretty young lady came aboard the bus and zeroed in on me. Before I could figure out why I was receiving this bizarre attention, she leaned over and asked in a hypnotic voice, "May I have your seat? I am preggers."

I snapped to attention and gently lowered the beauty into my ex-seat. Curiosity swirled around my head for a brief few minutes and of course the mandatory question rolled out, "How long have you been pregnant?"

Not missing a beat, our reposed cutie replied, "About half an hour, mate, and am I tired."

I stared out the traveling window as a tough smoke took over my face.

North to Spitsbergen

You have ten million miles of world travel under your belt. You have stood on the soil of 197 foreign lands. You yearn to see fresh horizons on the outer limits of the earth. You focus on the top of the globe and consider Spitsbergen, that rugged mass of islands lying far to the northwest of Norway and just a few hundred miles from the North Pole.

That is the Northway I went.

Since AD 1194, when the Vikings recorded its discovery in their Ice Sagas, Spitsbergen has drawn explorers, adventurers, whalers, miners, and fur trappers to its ice-sheathed domain in the High Arctic. In early summer when the ice fields begin to fragment under the 24 hours of daily sun, the polar-bound voyager sails out of Tromsö, Norway, aboard a tough little supply ship that shows the scars of many seasons of battling the Arctic ice. The deep eons-smooth shores of stone point seaward through the fjords, those fingers of ocean that spread inland along the coast. The ship bow swings north and the quiet of the Norwegian Sea hints not of the cruel days of World War II when dive-bombers operating from

North Norway's occupied airfields decimated Allied shipping. Those were the days when as many as 24 ships of a convoy of 32 to North Russia were sent to the icy graves of the Arctic seas. As terrifying as the attackers' bombs was the paralyzing cold of the sea itself. Today, shipping crawls across the undisturbed waters; here a fishing vessel, there a coal carrier.

Two days' cruising from the Norwegian coast brings the far-northern traveler to his first view of the lonely sea mountain, Bear Island, isolated in the fog and ice. Its shaggy face of stone and snow looms on the horizon as the hardy little ship works up the west flank of the island while it dodges the larger sheets of ice that now appear in its path. Bear Island is Norwegian and was discovered in 1596 by the Dutch explorer Willem Barents whose expedition encountered a polar bear when the first landing was made on the island. Today the bleak stone fortress is home for only a handful of men who operate a radio and meteorological station in aid of navigation. Up on its rugged cliffs a seabird population of many thousands nests in noisy comfort.

Now the ship cuts power and eases into a loose, heaving field of drift ice that stretches to the horizon. With booming and scraping, the foot-thick ice splits across the ship's bow and grinds down its sides. Inquisitive seals pop up and study this smoke-snorting intruder while dozens of gulls, ducks, and auks dive across the vessel on inspection flights. The drift ice eases off to reveal patches of dark blue water, and June's mid-night sun makes a dramatic entry out of the stormy sky. The waters around us become placid under the permanent sun which now dominates this seascape.

Fellow passengers include a glacier-climber, an ornithologist, fishermen, and coal miners. They take up positions on the bow for a first glimpse of the peaks of Spitsbergen. Translated, Spitsbergen means sharp peaks; Norway has another word for it: Svalbard, which means land of gold coasts. Norway assumed control of this island group under international agreement in 1925. Then, off to the right, shadowy in haze under constant sun, stand the majestic mounts of this lonely corner of the world. The peaks are in the 4700 feet range and are situated in the Hornsund region. Winter's grip is still evident as snowstorms and thick ice formations flash in the streaming sun. Ocean's blue gives way again to ice chunks, and the ship slows to a compatible pace, swerving first northwest, then northeast through the opposing ice floes like a football broken-field runner.

We halt at the entrance to the huge ice fjord where we lower supplies to a waiting boat from the radio and weather stations located at this bleak but strategic outpost. The few men stationed here are cut off from the outer world for most of the year, and the supply ship's arrival is welcomed warmly. Thanks to the warm drift of the North Atlantic Current, Spitsbergen's west coast is freed of its ice shelf for a few months each year. This current also moderates the climate for the same west coast where the principal settlements are located. Here the temperature drops to minus 34 degrees F and the summer temperature "soars" to about 40 degrees F.

Our destination will be Longyearbyen, the largest settlement on Spitsbergen and a coal mining center named for American engineer John Longyear who operated his mining enterprise from 1904 to 1916. Floe ice in the sea buffets our ship, and after hours of searching for an opening, we are met by a Norwegian icebreaker that comes crashing through the floes and leads us through its path to dockside. Coal mining operations are in full swing, and buckets on endless conveyor belts carry the product out of the mines directly to the docks for shipping. It is this highly efficient mine-to-ship transfer that makes Spitsbergen coal competitive with coal mined much nearer the great population and industrial centers of Europe and the Americas. Longyearbyen is a small community, principally Norwegian, operated by the coal mine firm. Some of the mine personnel have their families with them; their housing, community center, and church reflect a well-integrated life.

A few miles down the fjord is the large Russian coal mining installation at Barentsburg. Originally owned and worked by the Dutch, it was offered to the Norwegian government when the Dutch ceased operations. Norway was not interested in it, and the Russians purchased it, developing it into a large and important coalfield. Like the Norwegians' settlements, Barentsburg was destroyed in World War II but was rebuilt in the postwar era.

An interesting feature of Spitsbergen life is the efficient collecting of the large quantities of drift timber that pile up on the shores. By the time it arrives here, it has undergone an epic voyage from North Norway and North Russia. This prized timber is first picked up on its native shores by the ocean currents that sweep it up into the high latitudes where the steel claws of polar ice grip it and haul it across the Arctic wastes. Perhaps years later, this valuable wood is released by fragmenting ice on the shores of Spitsbergen. Since the island's only trees are but inches high at maturity, this drift timber is of immense importance in construction projects. The "trees" of Spitsbergen are polar willow and dwarf birch.

Geologists have been intensely interested in Spitsbergen, and expeditions from many countries have investigated the composition of its mountainous islands, which range in age from the pre-Cambrian to the Quaternary. In the summer months, once the winter ice shield starts its retreat, one can probe the glacier faces and discover fossils that speak of animal life and weather conditions eons earlier.

In World War II, Nazi troops occupied the islands after blasting the settlements with shells from warships. The Norse miners were safely evacuated beforehand by an alert system of continuing normal communications with the outside world without reference to the high state of alarm that pervaded the communities. These civilians were cleared swiftly and efficiently from the islands and were sped by ship to the safety of Scotland and England. Most of the evacuees returned to Spitsbergen after the war which also saw the Russians flee to Arctic Russia.

After a day at Longyearbyen, our little freighter steams out the ribbon of blue water through the ice and points its bow northward again, a puffing small bug on the sea, arguing its way across the ice floes. Off to the right, the hulks of Arctic mountains glitter their fiery green through sun, ice, and snowstorms. Down their valleys flow those glaciers, immense rivers of ice that grind and crash their routes to the sea. Massive blocks of glacier break off and crash into the ocean with deafening explosions that rumble across the polar stillness. A day's steaming takes us to a coal mining station at King's Bay where one is surprised to find a town of several hundred people who rate their homesite, Ny-Ålesund, the world's most northerly community. It lies at North Latitude 79 degrees. To give you an idea of just how far North that is, consider Stockholm at about 60 degrees North, or Chicago at about 42 degrees North. The Arctic Circle is 66 1/2 degrees North.

The long winter night that lasts about four months descends on these Arctic folk in autumn, and the midnight sun appears in spring for a day-and-night spectacle that runs until August. Reading, card-playing, making conversation, listening to radio, watching TV, listening to records, tapes, hunting, and fishing are some of the townspeople's diversions.

It was from Ny-Ålesund in 1925 that Norway's beloved Roald Amundsen, who was the first to reach the South Pole (1911), attempted to lead two airplanes across the North Pole. One craft was abandoned in polar ice and the second one was used to bring all members of the expedition back to the safety of Spitsbergen. The first dirigible crossing of the North Pole was to wait for one more year. In 1926, Amundsen, Umberto Nobile of Italy, Hjalmar Riiser-Larsen of Norway, and Lincoln Ellsworth of the U.S.A. made the triumphant first crossing of the pole in the airship *Norge*. Casting off from their mooring mast at Ny-Ålesund, they crossed the North Pole, and after 80 hours of flight, crash-landed at Teller, Alaska. The *Norge*'s mooring mast still stands at the Ny-Ålesund shore in silent tribute to these polar air pioneers.

In 1928, the Italian airship builder, pilot and explorer, Umberto Nobile, undertook a new series of flights over the unexplored polar regions in his airship, *Italia*. He again crossed the North Pole, but, on his third flight of exploration, the *Italia* was gripped in a massive Arctic storm and crashed on the polar ice pack. Nobile and seven of his companions were eventually rescued, but the catastrophe took directly, or indirectly, 17 lives, including that of Amundsen, who was lost in the air search for the stricken *Italia*. In an amazing encounter, I visited Nobile in his Rome villa some years ago, and heard his first-person description of these epic events in the dangerous polar air. He died in 1978, aged 93 years.

With reference to the 1926 polar crossing by the dirigible *Norge*, under the pilot-navigator Umberto Nobile, I was startled to hear from Nobile himself that as the *Norge* approached the pole, Amundsen ordered total radio silence that was actually observed through the polar transit, and until they flashed the signal of their success from Alaska. This break in communications, coming at the most critical point of their dangerous flight, created an international wave of anxiety that exploded in relief and joy when the crew radioed its victorious message.

Rear Admiral Richard E. Byrd, America's polar flyer and explorer, was the first to take airplanes over both the South and North Poles; he used Spitsbergen as his jump-off point for the northern transit of 1926. With air veteran Floyd Bennett as his copilot, Byrd took off from King's Bay, flew to the North Pole, and returned safely to their takeoff point after the historic transit.

The tragedies met by some of these air explorers at the dawn of the air age are focused by the daring Swedish expedition of S. A. Andrée, who boldly attempted a crossing of the North Pole by balloon in 1897. This was a highly organized project against heavy odds. A balloon hangar was constructed at the cast-off spot, Virgo Harbor, in the northwest corner of Spitsbergen.

Scrap iron was brought in, and when it was exposed to sulfuric acid mixed with water, the resultant hydrogen gas filled the great balloon for its electrifying, ill-fated flight. Andrée, his crew and his craft disappeared into the sky, and nothing was seen or heard of them until some 30 years later when debris and skeletons found on the little island of Kvitoya, far to the northeast of Spitsbergen, told the bitter tale of man braving the unknown polar skies in a powerless balloon. They had been destroyed by the savagery of storms and the immensity of the Arctic.

This traveler crawled through the waist-deep snow to the site of Andrée's hangar and found building timbers and scrap iron in abundance, remarkable preserved in the purity of the Arctic air. They had bade farewell to Andrée in the nineteenth century. A pyramid of stones gathered from the nearby shore bears a plaque honoring Andrée; it was installed by a Royal Swedish expedition in later years and stands as an enduring salute to the courageous balloonists. Scattered about the steep shores of Virgo Harbor are old graves that mark the end of life's travail for some of the Russian, Dutch, and Scandinavian fur trappers and whalers who competed for their fortunes in these waters in the last century. Spitsbergen's animal population includes seals, polar bears, reindeer, musk ox, hare, fox, and walrus.

After ten million miles of work, travel, study, and adventure in some 197 foreign lands, this is one voyager who finds that our planet reserves its ultimate grandeur for the Spitsbergen Arctic pilgrim.

The Attitude Adjustment Hour

Up on the tropical coast of New Zealand's wondrous North Island, I was seated with the fellow fishermen in a thatched hut that was in reality a beach bar. The booze was ice-chilled and most welcome in that warm, soggy climate. As we relived the day's catch of tuna and shark, my eyes slowly adjusted to the interior light. The bar was rustic, uncomplicated—no price labels or advertising. However, I eventually made out the lettering on a well-seasoned ship plank that leaned against a rum bottle. It bore this pithy comment on the Human Condition:

From 4 to 5 — Grumpy Hour = 5% off Drinks
From 5 to 6 — Attitude Adjustment Hour = 10% off Drinks
From 6 to 7 — HAPPY HOUR = 15% off Drinks

Money Terror

I was based at Athens, covering dozens of our Middle East and African Embassies for the U.S. Diplomatic Courier Service. Kuwait City was a favorite layover point because our hotel was away from the city, out along the gulf, and its swimming pool was cool and refreshing after the blazing desert heat. Over a two-year tour of duty I got to know some of the hotel personnel and a few of the lobby shops people, one of whom was an attractive young Palestinian lady who managed a money exchange office. I routinely exchanged my dollars for Kuwaiti dinars at her shop, and in time I acquired the status of a "regular" customer. One blazing morning I stepped out of the heat into her air-conditioned money-vault. She handed me a very hot thimble of black coffee and we chatted as I bought my dinars. As I reached for the door to leave, she placed her hand on the knob and asked if I would be so kind as to stand at her shop entrance and admit no one while she ran an errand down the arcade.

I was still digesting her question when, zoom, she was out the door. I stood there, terror-stricken to find myself trapped as sole guardian of two walls of cash drawers, many open and dripping with huge denomination bills: British pounds, U.S. dollars, Swiss francs, German marks. . . . Gold and silver bars and coins dazzled menacingly from an illuminated glass chest. I pressed my face to the door, peering desperately for the only person on earth who could extricate me from this unexpected monetary prison. A gentleman with a briefcase tried to enter, but I waved him off and pointed to my watch: 5 minutes! He disappeared, and the longest five minutes of my life crawled by at glacial pace before I heard the familiar click-click of Madame Money's heels.

I wanted to embrace my savior as she marched confidently into her shop, gripping tightly in each hand even more massive rolls of world currency. "That was the most terrifying five minutes of my life," said I. "I decided to say 'No' to your order to stand guard, but I was not fast enough to halt you," I continued.

My predicament never gained her attention; with great charm she replied, "No matter. You are so kind." With that, the cute little spitfire dismissed me to my world of canvas pouches.

Toilet Teeth

There are some wonderful corners around the world where routes cross and U.S. couriers get together over a brew and a meal. Much useful information on routes is exchanged, and sometimes a following courier will bring personal mail from the home base to a man who has been on the road for a long time. DipCourier rendezvous are numerous but some might be mentioned: Galle Face Hotel, Colombo; Stiegl Braü Restaurant, Vienna; Harry's New York Bar, Paris; Raffles Hotel, Singapore; Wentworth Hotel, Sydney; Trans-Tasman Hotel, Auckland; La Cabaña Restaurant, Buenos Aires.

In selected ports, our choice of restaurant or hotel might also be the favorite of the British Queen's Messengers or the Canadian Diplomatic Couriers. On those occasions we often joined forces for drinks, dinner, and the inevitable storytelling that ensued. The incident I best remember from those grand days of hard travel and exotic tales concerned a Canadian Diplomatic Courier who was caught up in a hilarious but painful episode at the Vienna Airport. On his flight into Vienna, where he was to catch another airplane to Paris, he had stirred up the cabin crew by remaining in the toilet even though the "Return to Seat" command had been given. The steward pounded on the door, and at last Courier X emerged, pointing to his mouth and, with difficulty, mumbling that his top denture had fallen into the toilet. He added sharply, " . . . and I must have it back!" The crew members stared at each other, then at the gaping toilet hole, then at the hapless passenger.

He was rushed to his seat and belted in securely as the flight crew crowded into the galley for a pre-landing strategy session. After the Vienna landing, Courier X remained on the airplane and pleaded with the airport technicians to retrieve his denture from its ridiculous hiding place. The first question the plane's engineer had for him was, "Do you really want it again?" Yes, the mumbling courier wanted it back and soon . . . because his Paris flight was due to leave in two hours.

Aircraft specialists dutifully dismantled the toilet tank and gingerly extracted the wandering denture. Under the appreciative gaze of the toothless voyageur, they rinsed it with soda water. Courier X then swished the prized choppers in a glass of cognac and wrapped them in a napkin. Did he pop the denture back into his mouth? Not then. Courier roundtables in far and distant lands say perhaps.

Mysterious Time

Now that we have seen in print a very serious history of time, the moment has come to examine the practical means we have at our disposals to expand time. An ancient Oriental opinion is that a man lives 75 days longer if he eats something outrageous, and the wisdom of the tenet lies in the fact that such a man will spend those gratis 75 days roaming the earth in search of other exotic foods that will gain him further life extension into infinity. Have you noticed the great age of the Orient's wise men? I decided to extend my life span while in the tea fields of Ceylon where the tea was world class, but where the black beetle omelet almost removed me from this planet. I earned my 75 days but had to give back ten of them recovering my health from the sinister omelet. I decided to seek alternative life-extension routes.

One of these proved painless and suited my heavy travel time-zone skipping lifestyle. Falling into bed in Thailand after cruising five time zones and facing a flight departure in four hours, I trained myself to sleep faster. When I hit the deck after just a few hours' rest, my internal clock was satisfied; I had run off a respectable schedule of snooze.

My other ploy to slow down the crunch of unharnessed time rests on my desk. It is a simple device, but I believe in it. It is a 19 month calendar. Whether I deserve it or not, I turn over a new year every 19 months. Anyone could adopt this private time machine, but not everyone can handle the shock and envy of the 12 month calendar crowd. If age is just a frame of mind anyway, you'd be surprised what youngish tricks you get into once you're unshackled from the old-fashioned year.

The Swiss Alps

High in Switzerland's Alps I was urged to attend the village folk music and dance performance. Tradition and pride run neck and neck in the mountain communities, and the local citizens turn out to cheer on their relatives and neighbors as they sing and dance. It was a good decision. I shared a table with a large family, and after the cheese fondue and wine, the music began. Two qualities caught my attention. One was the bright vigor of these mountain people who breathed superior air and consumed excellent foods. The other was the intricacy of their regional costumes which reflected endless generations of design and history. The music was lively, and the foot tapping and applause told me the townspeople were having a good evening.

An intermission followed the initial music section of the program and the wine flagons made the rounds of the crowded tables. This corner of the Alps spoke Romansch, a Latin derived tongue that seemed mysterious to me but well suited to singing. Soon the dancers took the center floor of the old inn and nimble feet flew with the bright fabric in a beautiful display of art and spirit. When the exuberance finally wound down and musicians and dancers had retreated into the kitchen, a gentleman suddenly appeared and, basket in hand, glided swiftly and efficiently through the tables, collecting tips. I did not take note at the time, but this basket man disappeared the minute he had completed his circuit.

Perhaps ten minutes later, two pretty girls of the dancing troupe emerged from the kitchen stage door and bowed deeply as an accordionist played a fanfare. They each carried a basket and started to fan out among the tables on a mission of tip collecting. Their smiles turned to scowls; something had gone wrong here! Several men jumped to their feet and ran out the doors. Dismay and excitement filled the air. An imposter had stolen the evening's tips and the whole village was searching for him. He had taken his life in his hands by stealing from an entire town.

When I departed this hamlet, the culprit had not been found. But the innkeeper assured me: "We know our land, every mountain, valley, and road. He is just a drifter, but he doesn't stand a chance . . . we will catch him." With Swiss efficiency they no doubt did.

The Pyrenees Mountains Descent

When I at last could wangle some free time from the Paris Regional Courier Office, I decided to invest this break in an attempt to visit four tiny lands that we did not cover on our courier runs: Monaco, Liechtenstein, San Marino and Andorra. I reached the first three without a hitch, but the last, Andorra, gave me a jolt to remember. It was winter, and from my location in Southwestern France the only approach to that mountainous land was up a steep valley newly paved with deep Pyrenees snow. I rented skis and filled my backpack with bread, cheese and sausage before skiing through the French border post facing Andorra.

The Andorra border post was unmanned: the winter hours, none. Villagers said that if I wanted an entry stamp in my passport (highly recommended), I must go to the border guard's home. That rusty old official plunked his rubber stamp onto my passport and off I skied into a remote little land that thrives on isolation and difficult access. Andorran independence is assured and its seclusion veils an invisible but highly refined open secret, smuggling. It is held by experts in the field that if the Andorrans cannot sell you something, it is still being invented. It took me most of a day to ski up to Soldeu where I found the sort of miracle you'll find in high mountains worldwide, an inn that is also a tiny brewery, butcher shop, restaurant, and bed and breakfast.

I moved in. I ate with the family in front of an ancient hearth: roast lamb, potatoes, cheese, bread, and endless crocks of dark yellow wine shuttled across the polished grains of their old table. The children tipped their wine mugs too. As a favor to me, the parents shifted into French from their distinctive Catalan tongue which totally baffled me. The electric lightbulb has been introduced into Andorra but you get the feeling its usefulness is still on trial. Candles and hearth fires seemed to be holding the upper hand on my visit and I welcomed their warm, cheery glow.

Deep sleep that night in a feather-down bed was recuperation itself after the hard push 8,000 feet up the valley. A hearty breakfast of coffee, bread, cheese, and smoked sausage launched me on my return to France the next morning. Well provisioned with more cheese and sausage for the trial, I settled my account in green U.S. dollars, preferred by these alert traders, and Madame let me in on a small conspiracy. She had been asked to tell the Americano that the little bandage on his hand where the ski pole had worn away the skin was the most beautiful decoration her young son ever wanted to put on his own hand. I glanced at my Band-Aid and noticed that it was quite a distinguished bandage. It was made of brilliantly colored material, but the crowning touch was a flurry of stars that adorned the little strip. I pulled a small can of Band-Aids from my backpack and emptied most of them on the ancient table. At the sight of these stars falling before him, the little fellow buried his face in his mother's apron. I believe this is the internationally recognized sign of overwhelming joy. It made all of us very happy, and in that wonderful mood I left these good people forever.

I started from Soldeu under gray skies. Descending the valley was a huge improvement over the climbing, and I made good time and distance. I should have paid more attention to the emerging sun and its effect on the snow. Thirty minutes of brilliant sun in that pristine air would melt the snow surface; an hour of clouds and icy winds would refreeze these watery stretches. No other travelers were moving, and that prevented me from exchanging information on ski conditions. No wonder the border patrol went to sleep for the winter.

The sound of wood scraping on ice hit my ears. Then I was shipped into a sharp slide that put me at the mercy of a long belt of frozen melt that offered zero traction for a mere mortal coming down a mountain on two thin slats of wood. Now I was sliding and turning out of control. I could not get a grip on the surface, and my speed was increasing. The lethal ice patch then decided it had punished its victim enough and threw me off the main valley track into the packed snow that ran several thousand feet to the bottom of the snowfield. My ski poles went flying. First one ski, then the second, snapped free, and I went into a three-minute free snowslide. With only one way to go, down, I tried to contort myself into the form of a human snowplow. In this way I was able to steer somewhat to avoid the boulders and trees that, given my dangerous sliding speed, might have shortened my life span drastically.

The bottom of the snowfield came up fast, and as my speed slackened, I steered between a rock formation and steamed to a halt. Funny, the first sensation I felt was not massive relief at having survived the fall. It was the oxygen-rich air that filled my lungs here, far below the altitude I had so suddenly departed.

I was a quarter of an hour regaining my breath and building up confidence to look over my predicament. When I at last looked up at the route of my fall, I had a flash of fear. For a fleeting moment I thought I might be snapping out of a bad dream, but the scene persisted. It was too graphic for a dream: my body path in the snow, two other tracks made by escaping skis, that sinister sun blazing new pools that would freeze and trap unsuspecting man. I stood in a metaphor of survival, a snow and granite vault, and I was hungry! My well-worn backpack was still laced across my shoulders but the sausage and cheese inside looked like they had spent the winter in a cement mixer. No matter . . . I feasted on them and went to work looking for my skis. That search ate up too many hours but I retrieved both skis; the ski poles had departed to the Pyrenees netherworld and have never been seen again.

My fall had actually reduced the distance to the French border, but not under ideal traveling circumstances. I skied over to the Andorran border official's home for my passport's exit stamp, then received an entry stamp from the French. The man who had rented the skis to me was not home, so I sat on his cabin porch until he returned. I did not wish to alarm him about the condition of his skis by telling him the hair-raising story of my fall down the mountain, but I had to account for the missing poles. We came to a reasonable settlement of all charges, and I was soon lodged in a warm provincial inn that radiated waves of aroma, mostly of garlic and ground pepper. I dined well and dreamed that night of an ocean, not of salt water, but of rolling white-caps of snow.

With Dr. Albert Schweitzer at His Jungle Hospital in Africa

Long before he received the Nobel Peace Prize, Dr. Albert Schweitzer and his famed jungle hospital in Central Africa had become my prized travel objectives. But the location of his hospital at Lambaréné on the Ogooué River in far-off Gabon made it hopelessly inaccessible for a diplomatic courier maintaining intricate travel schedules. After a decade of African duty, a brilliant window of free time opened one fine 1962 day in the Congo. A mix of changed schedules and a holiday combined to give me four and one-half days to myself in Brazzaville. It is eerie to behold your totally prepared state of mind when a long-held objective looms at you. I immediately borrowed an embassy typewriter and wrote two letters to Dr. Schweitzer, one in French, the other in English . . . my admiration for his distinctions in music, philosophy and medicine had compelled me to seek him out and personally walk the wards of his unique hospital . . . as an old-pro courier I would try to deliver my message in person . . . I would be grateful for a simple cot and a few bananas . . . I would stay at the hospital but briefly.

I quickly bought a ride on the shaky old DC-4 freight and passenger plane that flew from the Congo to Libreville, Gabon. From Libreville I would have to hitchhike along the dusty road eastward more than one hundred miles to the Ogooué River. Then I would have to find some rivermen who would paddle me downstream to Dr. Schweitzer's hospital. Just eight hours after I had learned of my free-time break, I was in fact hitchhiking eastward on the Gabon road to the Ogooué River. The rumored bus service never materialized, but, in view of my tight schedule, I did not even pause. A lumber truck moved me an hour along my path, then a fish supply truck took me almost to the river. A school bus hauled me to a river town where I had no difficulty finding a small fleet of dugout canoes.

On the River

They were concentrated at a muddy point where five people dressed in gleaming white were negotiating dugout transportation. They were Japanese medical personnel en route to the Schweitzer Hospital, and I was fortunate indeed to share one of their craft on the bumpy ride down the muddy stream. All of us searched the shore for the first sign of our destination, and in focusing so intensively, we overlooked a solitary human figure who stood on the riverbank. There was a gasp from the dugouts when the figure raised his pith helmet and waved it in greeting. It was Dr. Albert Schweitzer with his trademark white pith helmet in hand. He had come down to the riverbank to greet his guests, and that he did with enthusiasm, shaking our hands and then picking up as much luggage as he could carry for the hike up to the hospital. I was immensely relieved, first, that my French language ability was competent in this great adventure, and second, that my impromptu visit was accepted as a matter of course by Dr. Schweitzer and his medical staff. He accepted my letters politely and immediately took us on a half-hour walking tour of the hospital.

At Albert Schweitzer's Side

The wards were neat wooden halls well filled with Africans, of whom a small percentage were actually patients. It was the custom that an ill person was accompanied by a group of relatives and friends who traveled across great distances to be at hand during the hospital stay. The doctor pointed out that this body of family and friends imparted important psychological sustenance to the sick; in addition, these travelers performed many of the basic hospital chores, such as food gathering, maintaining fires, cooking, and cleaning. These were forms of payment for the treatment received by the sick. The medical staff said one of the operating principles at the hospital was that everyone made a contribution for his treatment or his stay. To charge nothing would leave the impression that the treatment or the stay was nothing. The contribution reinforced the value of the hospital experience. One of our stops on the hospital tour was the operating room at which Dr. Schweitzer paused to show us improvements which had been permitted by the Nobel Prize money.

My cell was tiny, neat and draped with an anti-mosquito net. Fruit and water awaited me on a tray. I introduced myself to Mademoiselle Ali Silver, a longtime ally of Dr. Schweitzer, who took me to the other staff members, among them Madame Rhena Schweitzer Eckert, the doctor's daughter, and an American medical couple, Drs. Joel and Jean Mattison.

The atmosphere of the hospital was muted; wood smoke hung in the air which was filled with a low hum of native dialect and the ancient accents of roosters and songbirds. Mornings were busy with procedures in the operating room and sick call for walking patients. Leprosy, hernias, and intestinal complaints, including parasites, headed the list of native medical problems. An early evening meal was served at long wooden tables in a hall that contained no flowers. The doctor's reverence for life extended to plants that would not be sacrificed to adorn a dining table. Boiled potatoes, beans, and fried sardines comprised the meal; a good pilsner made the circuit of the tables in large dark-brown bottles. Eating and conversing were in progress as I noticed Dr. Schweitzer rise from his chair and walk behind the diners.

A Bach Recital in the Jungle

Turning to see where he was going, I was startled to find that I had put my right elbow into the small of his back just as he was seating himself at his tropicalized organ. This man of four doctorates had been one of the world's principal interpreters of the music of Johann Sebastian Bach when he turned to medicine and departed the musical salons for a hospital in the African jungle. Music filled the room as dusk settled over this unreal setting in a far corner of the earth. I wondered if I were actually present in this dreamlike moment. It was a flash of introspection I was to experience on rare occasions on Mt. Kilimanjaro, in Antarctica and in Venice.

When the doctor returned to his chair, a roundtable discussion took place in German and French. The hospital staff joined French, German and Japanese experts in an evaluation of X-ray pathology, that evening's theme. At the discussion's conclusion, Dr. Schweitzer went to his famed desk and wrote late into the night. His assistants often pleaded with him to take more sleep, but his objectives and his energies kept him bent over his desk far into the night. I walked slowly past his crowded study and watched a unique figure of the nineteenth and twentieth centuries bringing the accumulated wisdom of a long and gifted life to bear on long handwritten manuscripts. These writings hung in profusion from the walls and ceiling of his workplace. They would one day reach their public in the doctor's books on religion, philosophy and medicine and in his interdisciplinary concern for all humanity.

A Giant of Two Centuries

I strolled through the dark to my cell. A very blue dome of sky hung over the hospital. Wood smoke from the kitchen fires laced the air. The thumps, chirps, and babble of the night jungle seemed totally right. I could not sleep. I felt I was for once in my life in precisely the correct spot on the earth at the appropriate moment, witnessing the applied philosophy of one of the most gifted humans of two centuries.

The hospital routine clanked into a new dawn. I padded over to the dining hall for a breakfast of bananas, tea, porridge, juice, and delicious dark bread. Dr. Schweitzer and his staff extended warm "Bonjours" to me and to each other at the long table before quietly marching off to work. He and his team performed surgery and saw patients bedside and in a walk-in clinic. Cleaning, sweeping, and brushing seemed to continue all day as firewood and food were replenished.

Just before lunch I sat down next to the doctor who had taken a seat on the outdoor steps of his office. He said the Nobel Prize money had been crucial to the completion of his Operating Room Center, and he wondered if such a totally unexpected award had ever been put to such immediate relief of suffering humanity. He wore his traditional pith helmet, short-sleeved shirt, and bow tie. I was struck by the great size of the man's hands, they seemed to radiate the music, the medical struggles and the very real grappling with the world and man's destiny. Those hands spoke too of his building of wards in his hospital, of constructing pipe organs in European churches, of his own keyboard mastery, and of his exhaustive writings. He shared this thought with me: One could conclude that writing out lists of medicines and supplies and then assembling them for the long journey to Central Africa were tedious jobs of little inspiration. He and his wife found that these preparations and the ultimate organization of the hospital created order, beauty, and function out of chaos and imparted an aesthetic satisfaction similar to the artful conclusion of a great movement in music.

An Alsatian Memory

I told the doctor that we new visitors were surprised when he appeared at the hospital riverbank and, after personally greeting each of us, picked up a guest's satchel and carried it up to the hill to the hospital. He smiled and said that was an old tradition here in Africa, and in his old Alsatian village of Kayserberg where it led to an amusing incident: after seeing a friend off on a train, the doctor was walking along the train platform and leaned over to help an old woman with one of her suitcases. The woman screamed for the police in belief that this stranger was attempting to steal her luggage. The station police responded immediately only to recognize the eminent local citizen, and they reassured the lady traveler that her suitcase was in responsible hands. For her part, the lady was unimpressed with the local citizen or the police.

The evening meal was fried river fish called capitaine, green beans, boiled potatoes, dark brown bread, tea, coffee, and that robust pilsner brew. The postmeal discussion was less structured on this occasion; the guests offered opinions based on their medical experience and the doctor did not perform on his tropicalized pipe organ. He did, however, lift our spirits by recalling an incident when he was a younger medical student.

Students Schweitzer and Einstein

He and another friend, student Albert Einstein, were traveling from Ulm, Germany, to Basel, Switzerland, by train. At the Swiss border, a customs officer slowly examined their travel documents. Perhaps too slowly. After patiently awaiting the return of their papers, student Schweitzer nodded to student Einstein and suddenly opened his human anatomy kit. At the sight of two partially dissected adult male fingers, the customs officer thrust their documents into student Einstein's arms and bolted from their compartment. The two future world figures reseated themselves and continued their conversation which dealt with structure, mathematics, and logic in the music of Johann Sebastian Bach.

I Receive a Schweitzer Passport

Dr. Schweitzer heard that I was to leave his hospital at dawn; he came to my cell and asked me to join him in his workplace. "You will travel a great distance by water and land before you reach your airport," he observed as he wrote on a photo he drew from his desk. "I will give you my passport which can help you on your way." Here I was standing next to his worktable, the famed "Tisch in Lambaréné," a phrase he used to begin some of his books. The photo showed him working at this very table. In German he wrote:

Am Tisch in Lambaréné
Herrn Robert James LaPlante zum Gedenken
an den Septembertag 1962 in Lambaréné.
Herzlich, Albert Schweitzer

At the table at Lambaréné
For Mr. Robert James LaPlante in remembrance
of the September day, 1962, at Lambaréné.
From the heart, Albert Schweitzer

My return journey to Brazzaville, far to the south of the mighty Congo River, seemed too far and too risky when I climbed out of my mosquito net before dawn. The nurses gave me a portable breakfast and lunch, and I paid a modest sum as a contribution to the hospital for my stay. Away I went down the steep riverbank to the dugout canoes that are always bobbing in the river current. The rivermen took me upstream and put me ashore at a point where a bright orange dirt road came to an abrupt end. I paid them and began my big hike west.

It was well after sunup when an oil truck picked me up and moved me to a lagoon where a dugout took over, then a bus, a family car, and another rural bus and, yes, I proudly showed my Dr. Schweitzer passport to these benefactors. "Le Grand Docteur" was the living legend of the bush. A Gabonese United Nations employee diverted from his route a few kilometers to deliver me to the Libreville Airport seventy minutes before my flight to Brazzaville. Despite a mechanical delay to the airplane, I reached Brazzaville four hours before my disbelieving embassy friends sent me off to complete my diplomatic courier route at Lagos. As I neared Lagos, a favorite quote kept intruding: *Inveniam viam aut faciam.* I shall find a way or make one.

Billy Mitchell Would've Loved It

There is a time of day at most airports when you suddenly become aware of Quiet. People stop shouting and begin to converse. Terminal windows cease their rattling every two minutes with pressing jet airplanes. This hole in the sound wall occurs when the roaring flying machines have all come, and gone, and at this rare point in time they are usually out boring holes in the blue beyond.

It was at Milwaukee's great airport, named after beloved American airman Billy Mitchell. The moment of Quiet had arrived, and I was enjoying it, sunk deep in a terminal chair, awaiting my flight. A couple of airline employees drifted into a nearby check-in corner, probably relaxing before the flurry of flights and decibels resumed. I was barely aware of the trio, and I doubt that they noticed me, last in a sea of empty seats. Then, like a cameo portrait right out of Broadway, came a swinging *tip-tap-tap tippity-tap* bouncing off the stone floors and shoes of a pretty brunette who danced past her airline colleagues in a tap-dance routine, singing, "I am not a brainless ticket-taker, no, not I . . . I can dance, if I try . . ."

She danced in an arc and tip-tapped right up to her friends, ending the cute little performance with a deep bow. When I had retrieved my jaw from the floor, I broke out in uproarious applause, clapping my hands and shouting, "Bravo! Bravo!" Her surprise audience of one scared the living bejavees out of our shadow star, but Billy Mitchell would've loved it.

Chippewa Weather

Where Lake Michigan and Lake Huron meet at the Straits of Mackinac I worked summers as a student on an island that was home to a number of wise old Chippewa Indians. Listening to their personal and tribal reminiscences I could visualize some of the events they had witnessed long ago, even before the turn of this century. Once, a sick man had to be taken across the frozen straits to a St. Ignace doctor, but a dogsled was not available. His friends wrapped him in furs and placed him in a light bark canoe which they towed on foot through ice and snow to the doctor's office.

Before the great steel car ferries came into use, moving cars, trucks, trains, and people across the straits gap between Lower and Upper Michigan, the Chippewa hauled humans and goods across these waters in their native craft. I was always on the look-out for their comments on weather, a big subject in this northern pocket of the world. But they never had much to say about it. At last I asked my old friend Ogima (Chief) why he and his circle of elders never discussed the weather. There was a beautiful economy laced with wisdom in his reply:

Wild weather is the good weather of the high Indian.
Tame weather is the big weather of the low Indian.

I Saved Two Cypriot Lives

The historic island of Cyprus has long been one of my preferred destinations. Courier schedules were civilized, we stayed at a great hotel, and the predictably gorgeous weather topped off an unbeatable combination. Our hotel was located in capital city Nicosia where the notorious Green Line bisects the populace: Greek Cypriots right and Turkish Cypriots left. The bombed and battered buildings along this line attest yet to the powerful emotions released in the 1974 war between these two main population groups.

Carrying my diplomatic passport, I was given permission to cross the Green Line, and I occasionally took that stroll through history. I always got the clear impression that the short, savage war had just halted: doors open, windows half open, clothing and pots and pans scattered through the shops and dwellings that once held people but now could offer nothing more than one dusty cat. On this particular Green Line ramble, I wandered right into a serious yet hilarious rescue role.

I had ventured off the no-man's-land borderline of the Green Line, and in that deserted zone I was startled to hear urgent yelling from several voices. My walking pace quickened as I peered into shop after shop, trying to locate the source of the shouting. The commotion came from the back of a metal and wood building at which I stepped over debris and smashed plaster to push open a dilapidated door.

The yelling climbed in pitch as I swung the door, whacking a man against the wall in the process. This unfortunate Turk was not alone in the sawdust-caked cubicle. A very large lady was opposite him at the long end of a moving wood lathe, except that nothing was moving. These two unlucky people had somehow entrapped themselves in a classic Shanghai fire frill dilemma. If the lady tried to squeeze out of her corner, her movement put tremendous pressure on the sliding top of the lathe that had trapped the man right on his belt buckle. His screams were echoed seconds later by the lady's when his gyrations attempting escape sent the free-floating lathe top banging into her considerable girth.

They both shouted detailed Turkish escape instructions to me while I tried pulling them up and out or down and in, all the while telling myself that it obviously was possible to entrap two humans in such an unbelievable configuration, but just how in hell had it been done?

In the midst of my frantic, but futile, efforts to pull or push this loud duet to safety, one word flashed before me: Dismantle. Of course, I thought, we're going to tear this machine down. My newly acquired Turkish allies had not the least interest in my mumblings in a foreign tongue, but when I outlined a screwdriver and hammer with my finger in the sawdust of the bench, the man managed a nasty smile and pointed to a rolled-up carpet lying on a shelf. I snapped it open and tools aplenty fell out. A barrage of commands told me which bolt to attack first and which ring to whack off with the screwdriver. Your scribe followed his directions faithfully, and it was the gentleman of course who first stepped free. In an instant the large lady was liberated, and to this day I am puzzled by her fascination with a cheese roll that was still in her grip when she emerged from the tight pocket. The simultaneous entrapment of the two had caught her left hand, with cheese roll, under the lathe table. Despite the constriction and discomfort, she would not be separated from her snack. Released, she swept the morsel to her jaws for a triumphant bite, as I wandered off marveling at my rescue of two lives in one afternoon.

A Red-Hot Gooney Bird

One of my toughest diplomatic courier runs was the predawn junket that covered Germany, France and England and returned to starting point Germany in one day. Not because I and my diplomatic bags were flown at lightning speeds to airports in these three well-distanced lands. My means of transport was the beloved C-47, twin-propelled old lady that got U.S. civil aviation into the air in the 1930s under its civilian name DC-3. She flew through the wins and losses of World War II and acquired the endearing name Gooney Bird while commendations recording her marvels piled up in flying archives the world over.

May I digress briefly from my account of the predawn courier run to share with you one of the affectionate portraits that emerged from the DC-3's war record. . . . In China a besieged Nationalist headquarters flight crew jerry-rigged a damaged Gooney Bird that had to fly. Highest ranking officers and civilians were in danger of being trapped by the jaws of an onrushing Communist pincer. The battered airplane had only one intact wing. Furiously checking over the crashed fuselages and wing sections, the flight crew salvaged one good wing. However, the prized find was a couple of feet too short and belonged to another earlier model airplane, the DC-2. Not to be fed to the Red gunners over a mere discrepancy in airplane specifications, the crew bolted the DC-2 wing to the DC-3 fuselage. Before the last bolt was turned tight the old lady was packed to the rivets with VIPs and cases of vital state documents. No time for a test flight . . . this old girl had to fly, and that it did, saving the day again in a dark, dangerous corner of the world. That airplane is enshrined somewhere in the Valhalla of retired flying machines as the DC-2 1/2.

But, to return to my narrative. . . . My C-47 courier run through Europe in one day became tough and routine; I soon established my own pace. After lashing down my pouches, I would grab a seat at the tail section of the old flying machine where I had space enough to spread out the amazing reams of paperwork today's courier has to conquer daily. No more of that wrist-manacled pouch romantic stuff. My loads of diplomatic mail could run to 40 pouches totaling 1200 pounds!

The trip I want to tell you about started in winter predawn. We loaded up pouches, some military freight and several soldiers. Pilot, copilot, navigator and radioman comprised the crew. We took off from an old airfield that had once been a fighter base for Nazi planes and headed for Paris where I had a pouch exchange with our embassy communicators. After an hour on the ground, the steady old C-47 nosed westward toward England. Daylight came grudgingly over Europe in February, so it was semi-dark when we resumed our job of boring holes in the sky en route to Britain. I was looking forward to a nap just as soon as I had brought all my courier paperwork entries up to date following the Paris stop. Our airplane was not pressurized which meant that the oxygen level was far thinner than it was on the ground, so I had to push myself to stay awake while completing my record keeping. My fellow passengers, the troops, were slumped in the arms of Morpheus, getting some enviable shut-eye.

An acrid whiff of something hit my nostrils and snapped me to attention. Instinctively, I unbuckled my safety belt and stood. When my nose reached the upper fuselage level I felt a bolt of fear: smoke! Fire on an airplane is bad news, big-time bad news. The smell was powerful as I leapt to the tail door which burned my hand on contact. I laced a cargo hook around the door lock and yanked it open and there in the dark, hissing and glaring red like a stowaway dragon, was a large radio unit, disintegrating in an electrical fire that posed real danger to the ship. I slammed the door and went to the cockpit. As soon as I pulled open the door, the smoke hit the crew's nostrils and these well-trained flyers went into action all at once. "Radio fire!" I shouted.

The pilot nodded his recognition and started to adjust his controls. Two crewmen ran down the aisle to the tail section. One look at the glowing red radio unit told them we were in serious trouble. The fire emergency signal was sounded, and the rudely awakened passengers could hardly believe we were preparing for an emergency landing. Anti-fire canisters were emptied on the glowing radio set but the resultant fumes were awesome. Several of the plane's window plugs were pulled out to drain smoke from the cabin, and I took note of high-pitched grinding sounds coming from the rudder and elevator controls that ran the length of the airplane. The pilot was trying to take us down, but my own flying experience told me that he had his hands full coaxing this old Gooney Bird to do his bidding.

The intense heat of this big red-hot radio set was overheating the airplane's cable controls, and the resulting warping almost tore the craft away from the pilot's hands. He had to force this runaway flying machine to the ground, in one piece or else. . . .

Dotted across this northwest corner of the French coast are the lifesavers of the postwar years, the scarred yet usable fighter plane airstrips that were used in fierce combat by both the Nazis and the Allies.

The pilot of our wounded bird fought and wrestled his plane through a long battle that ended in a rough and merciful landing on one of these almost forgotten airstrips. We dove out the exits to assess the fire's threat to the fuel tanks, but they did not explode. Our radioman had sounded the alert, and a relief airplane was already chasing us. As we carefully checked over the very hot ship, the pilot stated that because of cable control damage, his airplane, technically, should not be able to fly. Don't tell the Gooney Bird that.

Tess Toomey Finds Admiral Byrd

New Zealand always stirred up in my mind's eye grand scenes of explorers and sled dogs shipping out to "the Ice," that last place on earth, Antarctica. My personal hero in the long procession of courageous men who cracked Antarctica's code of mystery and isolation was Rear Admiral Richard E. Byrd, first by air to the South Pole, and later a leader of numerous expeditions to the White Continent. I had always viewed Byrd's exciting career with envy and admiration, but as a phenomenon of history long before my day. When my courier routes finally brought me to New Zealand I went immediately to Lyttelton, the famed old seaport which was the gateway to "the Ice." I found musty old seamen's taverns whose walls were hung with photographs and drawings of famous sailing ships from the classic age of Antarctic exploration. Yellowed newspapers told of triumphs and tragedies, from Shackleton to Amundsen to Scott. When I lifted my eyes from the clippings and gazed through the tobacco-stained tavern windows, Lyttelton's ancient harbor lay there unchanged from its days of past glory.

In time I met Tess Toomey, vivacious and unpredictable, and a very popular member of our Hotel Waterloo staff. When I knew my schedule would bring me into Wellington, I would write ahead to Tess and suggest dinner and a visit to a dance club. Between dances one evening, I happened to mention my fascination with Lyttelton, Antarctica, and Richard Byrd. Tess flicked her beautiful dark hair, and in an offhand tone said, "Yes, Admiral Byrd is one of our favorites." I could hardly contain myself, "Our favorites? What are you saying?"

She explained that she had several jobs in the hotel . . . back office, sometimes reception, and occasionally coffee-tea server in the residents' lounge. More than once she had brought tea to Admiral Byrd where he had seated himself in the lounge after dinner.

"Richard Byrd in my hotel? . . . He actually stayed here? . . . When?" I stammered.

Tess quickly brought me up-to-date on the legendary explorer. Byrd was advanced in years but made sporadic visits to Antarctica as a senior consultant to the U.S. scientific community there. He passed through Wellington and the Hotel Waterloo southbound and northbound on these journeys. So, this pretty young lady knew my hero, and, yes, she would introduce me to him on one of his visits.

The Byrd Alert

My courier mind began rolling dates and schedules through the slot-machine reels in my head. If I could just persuade my courier supervisor back at homebase Manila to put me on the New Zealand run at the right time, I might actually catch Admiral Byrd on one of his trips. So Tess and I set up an instant-Byrd-alert scheme: She would look over the future hotel reservations for an indication that the great man was expected and then send me a postcard with the dates of the admiral's transit of Wellington. As the courier trips rolled past, I read up on Richard Byrd's exciting career, filling in the few heroics I had not already absorbed. One of these was his near-fatal encounter with oil fumes and engine exhaust when he wintered alone in the Antarctica interior in 1934. Concerning this sensational near-tragedy, a strange turn of events brought me face-to-face with one of the men who rescued Byrd.

The cute and dynamic Tess Toomey was that marvelous contradiction, a young lady with looks and smarts, a tomboy who loved to wear her father's fishing jacket and boots on angling trips along the shores of Cook Strait. She invited me to fish with her gang, which included Les and Freda Chaston. After-fishing snacks and drinks at the Chastons' home were old traditions, and I thoroughly enjoyed those grand days with my New Zealand hosts. As an ex-maritime radioman, Les had an exotic collection of electrical signal and recording gear in his home. When the occasional Antarctic-bound explorer would appear at the Chastons' popular home, Les would thrust a microphone into the traveler's hands, and quite often some startling first-person accounts of great events on "the Ice" would be captured for all time.

Enter Bud Waite

That was the setting one late evening when we returned red-faced and brine-splashed to the Chastons' comfortable hillside home. An American technician, Bud something or other, had just returned from Antarctica and was an old friend of this happy gang of fisherfolk. Over good New Zealand brandy, we rearranged the universe to the satisfaction of dedicated fishers and out came Les's microphone. "Bud, tell 'em about Byrd at Advance Base . . . some of these blokes haven't heard about you and Dickie Byrd. . . ."

Bud Waite accepted the mike and, as if on cue, picked up the line of conversation with enviable aplomb. He had been part of a support party at Little America, Antarctica, in 1934, when erratic messages from Admiral Byrd, wintering alone in the White Continent's interior, caused alarm. Something in the messages hinted at incoherence or . . . was it equipment failure? A roundtable decision was made: Dickie Byrd was in trouble . . . his legendary strength and self-discipline were deserting him in this precarious situation. It was far more sinister than mechanical failure . . . Richard Byrd was not himself. Was he ill or had he been injured? The small detachment huddled around the telegraphic receiver, scanning every dot-dash syllable for a clue to his physical and spiritual condition. Then, the eerie atmospherics of the south polar world garbled the weak signals and thereby heightened the tension. Our narrator, Bud Waite, sipped his brandy and went on. He and two of the men at the Little America base would make a dash by snow tractor through the howling polar wasteland to Advance Base some 123 miles across the Ross Ice Barrier. Temperatures went to 60 degrees below zero as the trio dodged deadly crevasses and forged ahead into polar darkness to their microscopic target.

A Classic Rescue

Another enemy, the screeching blizzards born in that coldest weather factory on earth, the bottom of the world, tore at them as they advanced. At last they roared up to Advance Base and found Byrd staggering in near collapse but alive. One whiff of the air in the tiny weather base told them what had happened to their commander: fumes from his stove and carbon monoxide exhaust from a power engine had nearly killed him. The severity of these toxic gases had disoriented this tough individualist who was not entirely aware of the mortal danger he had survived. Bud Waite and his rescue squadron nursed Admiral Byrd back to health, and all four men remained for two more months at the site, continuing reports from history's first Antarctic interior weather station. Byrd's book, *Alone*, 1938, expresses "everlasting gratitude" to his rescuers.

I was frozen in my armchair as this first-person account of a historic near-tragedy fell from the mouth of Bud Waite. I knew well the details of Byrd's close call, but I did not remember the names of his rescuers. I was never to forget his name again. We became friends and maintained a cheery correspondence for two decades. With the cooperation of the Chaston family, Bud Waite's Wellington recordings and those of other Antarctic explores have been contributed to the Byrd Polar Research Center at Ohio State University where they are preserved and accessible to research scholars and the public. We have Les and Freda Chaston's daughter, Dianne Chaston Sundblom, to thank for this priceless resource.

I was thoroughly inspired by Bud Waite's narration as I left New Zealand to continue my courier schedule. Tess realized that I had happened upon a rare friendship, one that would someday take me to the White Continent itself. She assured me that she would scour the hotel reservations for news of Admiral Byrd's next arrival. Hardly two months had passed when my mailbox in Manila received her happy note: "Bob, he's coming next month, the 8th . . . don't know how long he will stay or when he will return to Antarctica . . . don't miss him. Love, Tess."

Return to New Zealand

I had discussed my New Zealand scheme with my office, and that proved to be helpful when I stood before our schedule board with Tess's note in hand. The supervisor switched two trips that put me into Wellington on the target dates. I agreed to a later schedule switch that would repay a courier colleague who gave up his New Zealand trip so that I might go. Typical courier lingo in the mid-1950s: "I'll do a Dhahran/India run if you'll pick up my Saigon Detail." Our working camaraderie in the Manila Far East Regional Courier Office was the envy of the Courier Service at large.

Tess and I exchanged several more letters before I reached Wellington on schedule. Admiral Byrd was due the next day, but my courier schedule had me on duty away from the city for the entire day. Tess caught me in the hotel lobby that evening as the embassy car dropped me off: "He's arrived . . . his group just left for a government reception!" My cute little plotter was obviously enjoying every twist and turn of the Admiral Intrigue. Off we went to dinner and our favorite dance club where all the details of the "meeting" were reviewed.

Everything was in place: I had a one-hour task in the morning, securing a visa, and the rest of the day was free; Tess had assigned herself to the luncheon and dinner coffee lounge. All that was required was for Richard E. Byrd to take post-luncheon or post-dinner tea in the lounge before Tess Toomey would bring the full force of her sparkling personality into play to introduce me to the Admiral of the Antarctic.

A Belle of Fontainebleau

To be perfectly honest, that is what happened, almost. I waited until the last possible minute before seating myself in the dining room for lunch. The famous guest did not appear. Miss Toomey and I were disappointed, and considerably worried. But that was to be expected when you are trying to intercept a busy explorer who was constantly in motion between meetings and receptions in a city and land which had taken him to heart. That left us the evening meal, and we two co-conspirators prowled the lobby lounge for a glimpse of the living legend. Tess then remained at the lounge entrance where she could command a total view of all human traffic in that corner of the comfortable old hotel. Always attractive, she seemed just a bit more elegant today, in starched white and black. She looked as if she might have just stepped out of the Royal Apartments at Fontainebleu. I sat deep in a cavernous lounge chair surveying the evening dining world.

My head suddenly tilted up. Tess had scurried across the carpet to meet a sole figure who approached the dining room entrance. I recognized him at once: Richard

Byrd! A smile rearranged his features as he extended his hand. This was a familiar face: the coffee-lounge hostess he remembered from previous visits. She escorted him to the dining room and then flew to my almost hidden chair, "You saw him? Oh, I am so happy he is dining here tonight." My instant recognition of him did not surprise her.

The next moves in our plan would require me to enter the dining room, sit at some distance from Byrd, and be prepared to finish my meal and follow him into the lounge. Several hotel staff members were greeting the explorer as he attempted to scan the menu. They politely dispersed, and Richard Byrd dined in silent contentment. I did not want to miss my cue from Tess, so I ate lightly and adjourned to the coffee lounge well before he finished his meal. From my favorite nook, I smiled across the room to Tess who moved with beverages from chair to sofa to table. The mood was subdued, and the air carried a trace of cigar and cigarette smoke as the diners relaxed.

A Great Man at Ease

Admiral Byrd of the Antarctic walked slowly from the dining room to a large upholstered chair, accompanied part of the way by Miss Tess Toomey, Guardian of Antarctic Explorers. He seated himself and presently she brought tea and cakes on a brightly polished tray. They chatted briefly and appeared to have come to an agreement about something. She then came to me and whispered: "I'll take you to him in a few minutes, when his tea has cooled." I was hugely impressed by my friend who was front and center in this small drama; she had become diplomat and social arbiter in one.

I wondered how approachable this man of action might be. Preoccupied or impatient? Cordial and responsive? My answer was telegraphed by Byrd's face as Tess led me through the lounge to his seat. He followed us visually, and before I could utter my prepared "Good evening, Sir," he extended his hand and waved me into the chair next to his. Our Miss Toomey faded from view, and there I sat, at elbow's length from the Antarctic explorer I had admired and studied since childhood.

No, I hadn't disturbed him. This was one of the few

quiet evenings of his New Zealand visit. He looked forward to his return to the Antarctic, and what was I doing in Wellington?

I handed him my calling card and said I was a diplomatic courier based in the Philippines. His expeditions to Antarctica, his first-ever flight to the South Pole, and in particular, the inclusion of Eagle Scout Paul Siple in his early exploring, had captivated me and given me two lifelong objectives: (1) try to meet Admiral Byrd face-to-face; (2) someday, somehow, place my foot on the White Continent itself.* I had that beaming Miss Tess Toomey to thank for the just-realized winning of goal number one.

He agreed that she was New Zealand's untitled ambassadress and then ventured into remarks on weather conditions he expected on "the Ice," the high quality of New Zealand food supplies for southbound explorers, and the great surge in postwar international scientific work he foresaw in the south. My object was to be brief, but he seemed to enjoy our conversation.

He spoke of the hazards and the panoramic beauty of the south polar flight and of the good men who had served with him on his expeditions. When I described my meeting with Bud Waite, one of his rescuers in the drama of the near-poisoning by fumes in 1934, Byrd brightened and recited these names as if he had just rehearsed them: "Waite, Demas, Poulter, and Charlie Murphy." Those men had pulled him out of serious trouble. They had also

*The Bob LaPlante foot landed on Antarctica in February, 1991.

made their contributions to history's first interior Antarctic weather station. As an old navy man from World War II, I almost saluted as I stood to leave. He surprised me by standing and offering a firm handshake, and away I went. Miss Tess Toomey, Guardian of Couriers and Explorers, loomed radiantly from an alcove.

Checking out the Berlin Wall, 1962.

Exotic Bangkok, Thailand.

The corps of diplomatic couriers awards the author (left). On right, colleague, Carl Bayard. Frankfurt, Germany, 1993.

The author worked on his manuscript in dozens of countries around the world. Stockholm, 1965.

Bob LaPlante is horn man with Tokyo Jazz Quintet, 1979.

Archaeology and Salmon trip to Labrador, 1978.

On summit of Mt. Kilimanjaro at 19,121 feet altitude, East Africa.

A concert in Sweden (left to right): John Fleming (Tenor) Bob LaPlante (Trumpet Aida) and Benet Bengtsson (Director), 1966.

Bob LaPlante at 10th Century Viking Archaeology site in North New Foundland.

Greenland Salmon, 1967.

The author helps tear down the Berlin Wall.

Greenland Abyss

A remote clearing of turf and stone that runs down to the sea in southeast Greenland holds fascination for me. It was first occupied and wrestled into the contours of a farm by that fierce old Viking, Erik the Red, way back in the tenth century A.D. Erik enticed a good number of Old Norse from Iceland to join him in this newly discovered land to which he attached the optimistic label "Green." Archaeological evidence bears out the accuracy of the old sagas, Viking histories, that say Erik's son Leif Eriksson left his father's farm, named Brattahlid, and reached North America in Newfoundland/Labrador about 500 years before that Italian gentleman Columbus skirted some Caribbean islands but never set foot on the great Northern Continent.

I have made several visits to Erik's ancient farm, but my last one nearly cost me my life. In summer when the heavy ice has crunched its way out of the great fjord that slices into southeast Greenland, the beautiful, wary Arctic char leaves the sea for its annual spawning run up the crystalline rivers of this huge ice-domed island. Here, then, you have the vibrations of Viking history as a backdrop to truly world-class sportfishing for this member of the salmon family. And you have it all to yourself. The Eskimo rarely tosses a line for char because his nets provide an easy, dependable harvest. In fishing the rivers emptying into Eriksfjord (his name is everywhere), I learned which ones were easy to reach and which were inaccessible to two-legged man. The reward for fighting through the medieval ice and boulders was to emerge from the Arctic jungle and find yourself directly above a wild pool of such great promise that you could "feel" a char's strike before you cast a fly. The sight of these great fish could grip your attention so tightly that you might forget the crucial details of foothold and balance, lest you fall off a cliff, or lose your fishing gear to the chasm always awaiting you below.

On my last foray into these char waters of the Ice Kingdom, my fishing had been untypically poor. Few fish were up the rivers out of the sea. Evenings I hung out at an Eskimo beer and darts saloon which had been created out of an abandoned airplane hangar. The friendly locals didn't think much of my nicked and scarred hands or my rod and fly apparatus. I usually kept my best fish for the day and contributed it to the camp cook. My northern brothers were invited to send one of their people with me so that I could send back several good fish, but that didn't appeal to them . . . too much bad country for a few fish.

I listened carefully as they told of the cycles of seasons, the phases of the moon and the movements of the char. I began to understand why there were so few fish in the rivers. At the last full moon there had been a rush of char upstream where they were now concentrated in the big pools situated in the hellish wilds of ice and boulders. The lower waters were nearly void of fish. I pressed the Inuit (the People), as the Eskimos call themselves, for details on these upstream pools. They laughed me off, saying that the country was blocked by gorges, brush and ice, and only the white-tailed eagle knew those waters and the great fish that swam there.

Nevertheless, I took my fishing rod and chow backpack to a promising valley and attacked the river route inland. In a couple of hours of rough hiking, I had left the fjord far behind me and started the cliff crawling I had expected. Now and then I could peer below to the river which indeed opened here and there into smooth, icy-blue pools. The boulders grew larger and the scrub bush turned sharper and thicker. Every fifty yards of progress was gained only through trial and error and retrial. At my planned angle of advance, I would break over a high point of stone and descend to the only pool I had any chance of reaching. After an inch by inch crawl, I edged up to the top and, careless with exhaustion, I made a mistake! The sight of several huge, colorful fish, rolling on the pool surface below, distracted me, and I lost my balance. I fell over the top, bounced four feet down the cliff face and landed square on my ass. My feet dangled over the edge of a boulder that had stopped me from instant death . . . but for how long? I was still sliding, with nothing to grasp and a downward tilting stone face slowly rolled me on ancient gravel to the mortal edge of the world.

Of man, may it be said here that it is merciful that he comes equipped with two buttocks. One would not have helped me in this extreme situation.

These two permanently attached seating devices are armed with muscles that have at least one priceless function: when you are sliding to oblivion over a Greenland abyss, tightening these muscles will "grab" the surface and slow or stop your slide. My slide sputtered to a stop . . . I stretched out my body for further surface contact and swallowed my heart! I was a long time putting together enough courage to check out the awesome mess I had gotten into. I had to get rid of these dangerous bits of gravel that had acted like tiny ball bearings rolling me along to my doom. I brushed them off my ledge and realized suddenly that they disappeared without any falling noise whatsoever. No wonder. My shelf hung several hundred feet above the river canyon.

My backpack was still with me; the fly rod had disappeared into Arctic eternity. I ate some smoked reindeer meat and bread and started inching my butt up the incline. I had to watch out for the wind which tugged at me in a low, hungry roar. Between tugs I cut my backpack straps and fashioned a loop that just reached around a rock outcrop. This solitary anchor returned my life to me. As I pulled and dragged myself to safety on my face, the words of the Eskimos rang out loud and clear; had I gone over the top of the cliff in that savage desolation, in a thousand years the only witness would be the white-tailed eagle.

Teddy Roosevelt

Cast in bronze is this plaque that hangs before the Panama Canal Headquarters:

> I built the Canal
> and the Argument began;
> the Argument runs on,
> but so does the Canal.
> Theodore Roosevelt

* * *

I often wonder if Teddy Roosevelt was the source of this pithy view:

> If Civilization demanded the resolution of every minute exception before moving ahead, Man would be mired neck-deep in the Ninth Century.

Aristotle Onassis

Aristotle Onassis, one of recent history's wealthiest men, had this advice for the young man seeking his fortune:

1. It is absolutely inviolable that you maintain a distinguished address: King's Court West, The Dorchester, The Waldorf-Astoria, even if you are the resident dishwasher.

2. Always walk slowly through the most elegant hotel or restaurant as if you were the new owner on an incognito visit.

A Diplomatic Spiking

Soon after my arrival at our Paris Embassy in the early 1950s, *the* event of the season was the ambassador's Fourth of July reception at his impressive official residence. This was always a grand time to be in the City of Light and I was off-duty between courier trips, so I donned my only dark blue suit and headed for this overseas American birthday party. French and American guards, in dress uniform, patrolled the approaches and the gates of the ambassador's residence, and dazzling weather enhanced the dignified atmosphere of the gathering which was well attended by American and European diplomats and officials. During the official Fourth of July ceremonies, I was startled to find myself elbow to elbow with Mrs. Franklin D. Roosevelt and Mr. James Farley, the late president's right-hand man.

The faint aroma of champagne wafted over the prominents while a string quartet played patriotic airs from America's past. Drinks and delicacies shifted from butlered trays to chatting guests; it was the epitome of diplomatic grandeur.

"Oww!" suddenly crackled across the defenseless

refuge of mannered people. To my left I saw an embassy vice consul standing on one leg and holding his foot as he yelled from the depths of his lungs. I rushed to his side and helped him to a chair in a lawn tent where he removed his thin shoe and sock. His foot looked like it had been charged by a .38 caliber slug that had tried to grab it and run away. He was getting hold of himself, "It was that 300 pound woman with the plumbing around her neck; she did it."

I raced out to the service table and filled a napkin with ice cubes. As I bound up his tortured foot in soothing ice, I asked, "Did what?"

He sputtered, "She backed up on me and speared my foot with one of those tongs she has on her feet . . . and do you know what she said to me when I yelled bloody murder? Some sort of party chit-chat like, 'It *is* nice, isn't it?'"

Calendar Time

Hurtling along through the time zones of the earth, couriers adapt to many quirks of culture, weather, and means of transportation. I hadn't realized how well I had adjusted from Pakistani horsecarts to Hong Kong freight canoes to jet airplanes until I found myself one day on the old four-propeller workhorse that flew from the Panama Canal Zone to an air base in Florida. I knew it would be a good ten hours before we droned through the Caribbean skies to that airstrip in West Florida, so I settled back with Roald Amundsen's thick and exciting *The South Pole* and let the clouds flit by.

My seatmate, a young army private first class, was all excitement. This was just the second airplane he had ever boarded, and this was his first chance to go home since being assigned overseas. We chatted and devoured the box lunches which the air force distributed to us. We took turns reading sections of an old copy of *The Stars and Stripes* military newspaper, but our homebound soldier really had interest in just one thing: he wanted to shove that slow, old airplane through the skies to the U.S.A. as fast as he could. I resumed my reading, took a nap and later opened my briefcase to rough out my trip report. Then I heard the private say, "Sir, when are we going to get to the States?"

I happened to have a courier schedule calendar in my hand, so I laid it out on our armrests and started to say, "Let's see, we got airborne on the 10th," and as I ran my finger along the dates, he grabbed my finger and covered it up.

"No, don't look at that calendar," he gasped, almost in terror. "We're going to get home by clock-time, aren't we?"

We did.

A Freudian Slip

Sigmund Freud held, among other views, that man does nothing by total accident; the unconscious reveals his true motives.

In Freud's Vienna, I had at last gotten to know the gorgeous, sensuous Sabine, a dancer who was also a published detective-story writer . . . the plot already thickens. One wintry night, following her theater performance, we were having a late supper, as show people like to call it, in my hotel restaurant. This was as close as I had yet been able to entice this magnetic young lady to my hotel room. After leisurely dining and enjoying the superb Danubian wine, Sabine thought she would smoke a cigarette. I reached into my pocket for a book of matches, but as I withdrew my hand a sparkling blue packet of condoms flipped onto the floor. The cool lady smoothly scooped the condoms from the carpet and placed them firmly in my hand. She said she would not like to smoke her cigarette just now . . . perhaps later in my room.

Yes, this was Vienna, I thought . . . it's all Freud's fault.

Sergeant Ohlsson

There I was, gassing along in my old Volkswagen Beetle, pushing it to the limit as I clung to a road along Sweden's Baltic Coast. I was late, dangerously late, for a crucial train departure from Stockholm to the Arctic. Two years' planning had gone into this chance of a lifetime to train up to Narvik, Norway, and bus over to Tromsø where I was to board an old sloop for the unpredictable run to the near-top of the world, Spitsbergen.

Everything fell into place in this elaborate international mosaic except the clutch on my old black VW which decided to end its life on a wild stretch of Swedish forest. I had almost decided to get out and hitchhike into Stockholm when a farmer appeared and towed me behind his small truck into a village. It was nighttime, and the town was buttoned up tight. It should have been dark, but here in June the midnight sun kept traveling in a low arc across the northern sky, never setting.

I slept in the car, parked in front of the mechanic's house, a wise decision by the thoughtful farmer-savior. In the morning a young man, two girls and a cat came out to inspect the night's gleanings. A sick car is not a surprising revelation on your doorstep when you are the only vehicle-doctor in a Swedish village. Some years before I had done graduate studies at the University of Stockholm; this permitted me to sketch out my plight in Swedish as mechanic Ole and his kids led me into their kitchen where his wife greeted me and offered very welcome coffee and hardtack, the Scandinavian crispbread. Ole was on the phone briefly, and I listened intently for the tone of voice or key words that would tip my fate. Calm prevailed; the clutch parts would be dropped off at a nearby gas station in about two hours. The mechanic would install them in my VW right where it stood in front of his house, about a two-hour job. He thought I should be on the road to Stockholm in maybe four hours.

And that's about the way those four hours passed. He did a superb job of clutch replacement and carved precious minutes from my time-squeeze in the process. I paid up, thanked one and all, and roared off for the capital city and its irreplaceable train.

Like so many tight predicaments I get into, parking the VW and catching that train were just about impossible in the fast disappearing minutes before departure. Still, I bore on, making the train station the first, the only objective. My familiarity with the city's medieval streets and back alleys proved most valuable as I snaked my way to the terminal. I refused to even glance at my watch, but when I at last steamed up to the station plaza a huge black and white clock shook me to the marrow: it shouted at me, "SIX MINUTES TO DEPARTURE!" My polar odyssey hung by the narrow thread of 360 seconds.

Out of this maelstrom emerged a blue-clad Viking rescue mission in the person of a young police officer. I jumped from the VW, threw my Arctic gear on the cobblestones, shoved the car keys into his big mitts and said I had only five minutes to catch that Polar Express I was an explorer on the trail of Andrée, Amundsen, Peary and Nobile. "If I miss that train I will lie down and perish right here on the cobblestones of Stockholm . . . here, use my car . . . I'll see you in a month."

The young officer did not require pictures, graphs or illustrations. He smiled understandingly and uttered just four words, "Ask for Sergeant Ohlsson."

I zoomed into the terminal, caught that train with 40 seconds to spare, and sat on my Arctic gear in the corridor for 200 kilometers (120 miles), slowly digesting my close call and the miracle of Sergeant Ohlsson. I did reach Narvik, then Tromsø where I boarded an old supply sloop for the ice-dodging voyage to mystic Spitsbergen, deep in the Polar Arctic. The journey had a lifetime imprint on me and has led me to other high Arctic destinations from Greenland to Antarctica. It also led me to a Rome villa where I was astonished to discover, still living in the 1970s, General Umberto Nobile, the navigator-pilot who carried Roald Amundsen (first at the South Pole) across the North Pole in the dirigible *Norge* in a 1926 flight from Spitsbergen. Hearing this event from the classic age of polar exploration explained by the man who led one of its greatest discoveries is one of my never-to-be-forgotten privileges.

One month after my riotous departure for the North I walked up to the Stockholm Rail Station police desk and asked for Sergeant Ohlsson. Old friends by now, we shook hands warmly when he appeared and sat down to coffee at the adjoining cafe. No, he wasn't too shaken by my frantic car-disposal scheme; he'd seen many crazy last-second antics in front of the terminal. He told me about one of his fellow officers who had to accept a Lapp wife nearing childbirth as her husband rushed off to the Arctic to save his wolf-threatened reindeer herd.

After the sergeant's duty shift, I rode the bus with him to his suburban home where I had difficulty recognizing the shining black and chrome VW that bore my license plates. Son and daughter had slapped some Swedish spit and polish on my old wheels which never looked better, glittering there in the midnight sun. My gratitude for this family's instant hospitality has never ceased. I made a deposit in the children's piggy banks, and I later wrote a letter of commendation to Sergeant Ohlsson's superiors on my official stationery. But nothing can capture the beauty and the excitement of the train that almost got away.

Five Reasons We Should Drink

Handpainted on the wall of an ancient pub in Colombo, Sri Lanka, is this honest reflection from the seventeenth century:

> If all be true that I do think,
> There are five reasons we should drink—
> Good wine, a friend or being dry, or
> lest we should be by-and-by, or
> Any other reason why.
>
> — *A Catch*
> Henry Aldrich 1647-1710

Burrhead

Burrhead Robinson was tough. You didn't need personal details about Robbie to gain the distinct impression that here was one indestructible hombre. I met him at the end of World War II at the University of Michigan where we were both GI Bill students. When he tried out for the renowned Michigan Wolverines football team, the backfield coaches could not believe their eyes when they saw this young Kentuckian's strength and speed. How had such athletic talent escaped the tight recruiting net that all college football powers spread across the land each year? The war was the answer. A legion of college age football powers had joined their fellow citizens in the military service and had disappeared from sports for several years. Some of these young men survived combat duty and battle injuries and returned to school at war's end as older, much more mature students. Burrhead Robinson had been a gunner on a B-24 Liberator bomber that was nearly bisected by Nazi fighters' gunfire over France. He parachuted into a mountain village and was pulled through the French Resistance pipeline to Britain. Here he was now, mowing down football players as a brilliant pass-blocker on a Big Ten Championship team.

Robbie loved his old Kentucky home, and before his football fame took hold he would hitchhike there during school breaks. On his return from one such home visit, he told me about a hilarious encounter with one of his Kentucky countrymen. The older gentleman stopped his pickup truck for the student hitchhiker, and after a few miles of easy chatter, the driver said "Son, open up that glove compartment and hand me that pistol and the jug of bourbon." Robbie popped the glove compartment open and sure enough a handgun and flask of bourbon greeted his eyes. He handed both curious items to the old gentleman who, passing the bourbon back to Robbie, said, "Have a snort!"

Athlete Robinson took a careful look down the barrel of the gun and replied, "Oh no, Sir, I'm in training . . . I play college football . . . I can't drink any bourbon."

The old-timer then held the pistol on his passenger, and in a commanding voice said, "I said, have a drink!"

Athlete Robinson took a careful look down the barrel of the gun and replied, "Well, you know, I'm a good old mountain boy myself and I know homemade whiskey. I think I will have a sip," as he tipped the jug for a drink. Robbie said it was god-awful rotgut, bad moonshine.

As he was recovering from the devastating taste, the truck driver said, "Here, you hold that pistol on me and now I'll have a snort!"

The President's Diplomatic Courier

I waded into Washington, D.C. at an exciting time for a rookie diplomatic courier freshly armed with a GI Bill university diploma. It was the autumn of 1950, and I was hardly enrolled in a Foreign Service training class when the power center of the earth, the corner of Pennsylvania Avenue facing the White House, exploded with violence and terror. Two Puerto Rican Nationalists mounted a bloody attack on President Harry Truman's temporary residence, Blair House, that resulted in the deaths of one presidential guard and one Puerto Rican assailant. Two guards and one attacker survived gunshot injuries. The president and his family, upstairs at the time of the assault, emerged unscathed. They resided at Blair House, the official presidential guest house, during the long overdue renovation of the White House which stood directly across Pennsylvania Avenue.

This shattering event caused many a missed beat in the throb of the capital's life. When I entered my favorite drugstore on the corner opposite Blair House two days after the shooting, I saw two new additions: an ugly bullet hole through a front window and a newspaper story plastered next to it describing the tragedy. Momentarily,

I wondered if the fast-food counter at the back of the store was becoming just too dangerous. Come on now, said I, after firefights on the beaches of Okinawa, this is just political gun slingin'. Besides, at my fragile salary of $3110 *per year,* I was not about to be run off an economic meal source. I finished the foreign service training course and received my first diplomatic courier assignment, a long three-week run delivering and accepting diplomatic pouches at 23 U.S. embassies and consulates throughout Latin America. The trip went well, although a lightning bolt that shook my Pan American Constellation over the Caribbean Sea made me wonder if such a shock were routine or deadly serious. I never could get a straight answer to that question.

The last flight legs of my inaugural courier run went from Argentina to New York City where I switched my pouches to a sleeping compartment for the overnight train to Washington. I crammed the leather and canvas bags into every corner of the compartment, but one still ended up on my already stingy bunk. Off we chugged for the nation's capital.

In the morning a knock at my door brought a welcome cup of hot coffee from the train porter. Before I could wedge the door closed, a man close behind the porter held a government agent badge in my face and said that on arrival in Union Station, Washington, D.C., I would have to remain in my compartment for about 20 minutes before disembarking. Government business! I immediately handed him my diplomatic passport and said that my pouches had to be delivered promptly to the Department of State. He looked the passport over, carefully studied my face and said he would return in a few minutes. A second man accompanied him on his return. They re-examined me, took note of the diplomatic pouches, and said that I would be permitted to leave the train immediately on arrival. They would make arrangements for a station porter and baggage cart to move quickly through the terminal. Within minutes of our arrival at Union Station, a safari marched down the deserted rail platform: one station porter pushing a baggage cart piled high with diplomatic pouches, one diplomatic courier and two U.S. agents. It was early, seven in the morning, but it seemed too quiet, too subdued, even for a Sunday morning. As our tight little convoy reached a point where the platform meets the main station plaza, we passed close to a huge black limousine that had somehow gotten permission to park in that privileged spot. I got the picture very rapidly when I recognized the famous figure who stood at an open door of the Cedilla. I turned my head and boomed a "Good morning, Mr. President!"

President Harry Truman smiled broadly and in his very personal Missouri tones, replied brightly, "Good morning!"

Noted for his early morning strolls, this president was on hand to welcome his courier home from a tough, first overseas mission. Yes, that was it. The Diplomatic

Courier Service must occupy high status indeed if the Chief Executive himself takes such personal interest. This happy frame of mind lasted about a full three minutes before I was flattened by the news that Mr. Truman was really on hand that morning to meet his wife and daughter who were aboard my "Courier Train."

The Steal

The ancient village of Sachsenhausen has pondered the fate of humans for longer than twelve centuries as it clings to the banks of the River Main just opposite Frankfurt/M. Its jaunty atmosphere and renowned food and drink might lie at the base of its popularity. Perhaps it's the old quarter's loyalty to the past, its unchangeable Saxon architecture, and its proud, cheery inhabitants. You feel this special mood the moment you cross the bridge from Frankfurt. Vehicles and humans slow down; there is more walking than driving. Some of Sachsenhausen's most interesting streets are closed to wheeled traffic except the horse-drawn wagons that still make deliveries to restaurants, shops and taverns. All the better to get close-up to the sausage stalls, the beer pubs ,and the apple-wine inns. Not to mention the rock and roll clubs and jazz bistros that wail every night.

The good, democratic folks of this venerable village sometimes bragged that they had never set foot in the big city across the bridge, Frankfurt; too far, too noisy, they said. But they heartily welcomed all visitors to their privileged town, and they wore with an old ease the prosperity this policy brought to them.

My entrée to this feisty community was jazz, which was heralded as America's contribution to the arts and was highly respected in its own right. As a trumpet player with the U. S. university jazz groups, I carried my horn along when I joined the Diplomatic Courier Service. Imagine my happy surprise when I was assigned to Frankfurt/M, a city with *four* jazz clubs. In time I played all the jazz stages and thoroughly enjoyed the music and my newly gained family of night people. However, serenity in music, or in life at large, rarely travels in a straight line. I learned that little lesson late one Sachsenhausen night.

I had joined a good swingtet for a great evening of music at the Jazz Coach, much favored by musicians because of enthusiastic audiences and the wonderful acoustics of the solid wood walls. Good times always fly, and one in the morning, closing time, was on us much too soon. We gathered up our horns and girlfriends and decided to move on to the Jazz Tavern which would close three hours later. You can see why the JT was much beloved by opera singers, late-night airline pilots, midnight shift nurses, and jazz musicians. Typically, on music nights I fail to eat dinner, or lunch for that matter, so I cut out for a snack and told the gang I would join them shortly at Jazz Tavern.

I squeezed into a hole-in-the-wall grill which was run by my old Spanish amigo Pepe. The aroma of charcoal grilled sausages, octopus, and shrimp was heavy enough to be shoveled, and the place was packed with the post-midnight crowd. Pepe smiled and automatically scooped up a platter of grilled shrimp and a mug of beer for me. I had to carry my trumpet case on my head to slide through the mob, but I finally came to rest before my shrimp and brew. The beauty of nourishment is that it is invisible. That mystical apparatus, the human body, will grab cabbage, pigs' feet, chicken wings, octopus arms, or oranges and secretly convert them to unseen energy. You can never identify the one man in 40 who will hike 150 miles through Antarctic wastes to rescue a marooned pilot. The body keeps its secrets well.

I regained my strength over Pepe's platter and thought of the great music that lay ahead. Sometimes jazz is called recreating music after midnight in dark, smoky rooms. We would have a few more hours to play at the Jazz Tavern. A brilliant Austrian tenor sax-man would be joining us so would Duke Ellington's ex-bassist. Exceptional line-up.

I paid my bill and pocketed a ten-mark note as change. The packed bistro looked impassable, but I placed my horn case atop my head again and started nudging bodies out of the way en route to the street. Two guys then sandwiched me, and I felt a hand in my left trouser pocket. "Why, that son-of-a-bitch is picking my pocket," said I, as I crunched my trumpet case from head-high smack on top of his head. Hard! As he buckled to the floor, my right knee caught his jaw in a classic KO crossover. My elbow had instinctively smashed into the gut of the thief on my right, but I had a fleeting expectation of a stranglehold, a knife or worse. None of these exciting events materialized because Creep #2 had climbed over the riot of humanity and was out the doorway. Pepe grabbed a wooden bar stool from me just as I was about to administer the coup de grace to crushed Criminal #1, totally helpless on the floor but still clutching my ten-mark note in his hand. The night people cheered and thumped me on the back as I opened my case and checked the horn for damage. Not a dent. But the case itself had a raw split along the side that had knocked the thief's head into the Zero Time Zone. My case still has that raw split; sometimes when I notice it, a nasty smile tries to take over my face.

I told Pepe that I had another gig at Jazz Tavern and would not hang around for a police report. He said to forget this punk . . . no cops, no ambulance . . . the dishwasher would dump him out the back door into the alley. Half an hour later we were blowing "Satin Doll" at the J-Tavern.

Wrong Identity

It was a barroom brawl right out of the frontier west, except that it erupted in the City of Light, in the feisty Pigalle quarter of Paris. Some U.S. GIs were on leave from their units in Germany, celebrating the wine, women, and song of this renowned district. An argument led to a fight, and Le Train Bleu was immediately engulfed in flying furniture and swirling bodies. The innkeeper routinely called the gendarmes. These lightning-fast men of the Pigalle Night Patrol pounced on the combatants and with great authority selected one GI as Chief-Trouble-Maker. They marched him a few blocks to their local station which, after eons of human conflict, had been established right in Pigalle.

Some of Chief-Trouble-Makers buddies followed the gendarmes and their detainee to the night station where the mysterious drama of gendarme protocol unfolded before their attentive eyes. They did not handcuff or otherwise restrain the Yank, but he was led to a well-worn chair that sagged sideways as he sat in it. A policeman at the desk removed a drooping cigarette from his lips and asked, "Francais?"

The GI replied, "No, I don't speak French."

The desk officer then switched to patrol-station English and asked for the soldier's Identity Card. The officer scribbled three sheets of misconduct during the next half-hour and, after lighting another smoke, suddenly stood up and handed the American his ID card and a carbon copy of the scribbling. He said, "That is all; you can leave."

The GIs crowded out the door of the patrol-station and gravitated quickly to a well-lit brasserie for a round or so of Pigalle night-potions. One of the troops undertook a serious review of the three pages of scribbling that detailed the great barroom brawl. He had a passing acquaintance with the French language, and his serious demeanor terminated abruptly as he scanned the pages. He broke into laughter and stunned his drinking buddies with the announcement that the police desk officer had not written up old pal Chief-Trouble-Maker. Unfamiliar with American ID Cards, he had penned a scorching indictment of the army officer who had issued the card to our barroom brawler. Freudian slip or Gallic justice?

Really Sharing

In the High Arctic I was befriended by a pretty Eskimo girl with the un-Arctic name of Salome. By days I worked on an archaeological site, and in the evenings Salome and I would join her friends in the village pub where dart throwing was the main event. Near the end of my stay, Salome pointed out Doris, her close friend, and said she wanted Doris to stay with us several nights, because she had not found a suitable boyfriend. It was their custom to share minor and major possessions and these included an understanding boyfriend. My archaeological education became secondary to a vast improvement in my grasp of human relations.

Instant Income

We met an unemployed jazz guitarist on the streets of Frankfurt/M, Germany, and invited him for a beer at the Jazzkeller. He agreed to join us but said this time he would buy a round. He admitted his pockets were empty, but he would nevertheless be able to buy a round. We took a table and listened to the music. The place was packed and now and then we would catch sight of the guitarist who left his jacket at our table and tucked a white towel into his belt. He had become an instant waiter. A round of drinks arrived, including a beer for the waiter who told us mischievously that he had gotten the drinks at "employees' prices."

Backstage with Duke Elfington

The Duke Ellington concert in Frankfurt am Main, Germany, was sold out. Radio and TV would cover it and the concert hall would be truly the scene of a great musical event. I had been away on courier travel and had not gotten a ticket. The day of the concert I telephoned Duke's Frankfurt hotel and was startled to be connected at once to the great musician himself.

I had played some jazz trumpet around Europe . . . had huge admiration for the Ellington Orchestra . . . would there be any hope for his speaking with his producers about tickets?

Duke listened patiently and said, "You can hear the concert backstage. Inform the band entrance personnel that you are my guests." That was all there was to the conversation.

I immediately alerted my girlfriend who passed on the good news to another courier and his girlfriend. We arrived early at the concert hall. I brought along one of my trumpets, and as we passed through the musicians' entrance I yelled, "Band," and suddenly we were backstage. The trumpet I had brought along is my Aïda trumpet which is five feet long but breaks down into three sections. I sought out trumpet soloist Cat Anderson whom I had known for years. He took a special delight in the trumpet Aïda and quickly devised a little plot which he would drop onto the band. He hid the three pieces of the horn under his band seat and would surprise his bandmates, the piano player Duke Ellington, and the huge physical and electronic audience at the appropriate moment. In the meantime we were permitted to sit on the corner of the concert stage itself . . . the best seats in the house, barely two steps from the musicians.

The great orchestra roared into its show opener, "Take the A-Train." Duke was standing next to us. He greeted us warmly and shook hands with each of us. I mumbled something about thanks for making it possible for us to get into the hall, but in the back of my mind I was worried. The band was well into "A-Train" and here was the piano player chatting with some offstage characters. With the calm and poise of half a century at the head of a great orchestra, Mr. Ellington suddenly swooped to the piano for the second chorus that could barely be heard above the explosion of applause from a huge audience.

Several pieces later, the band played a lush ballad that featured our friend, the mischievous Cat Anderson. When his trumpet solo came up, he assembled the five feet of trumpet Aïda from under his seat and slowly walked down the stage to the front-solo microphone. His bandmates had heard him play that solo so many times that they rarely took notice of him moving to the microphone. But when first Duke, then the brass players, then the reed section saw the shining five feet of trumpet Aïda swing to Cat Anderson's lips, there was a big laugh and a nice lift in the music. Spontaneity has always been at the heart of jazz.

Khyber to Kabul:
A Flash Flood at Jalalabad

The trail that took diplomatic couriers to the American embassy in Kabul, Afghanistan, was long a traditional adventure with strong Kiplingesque overtones. In the early fifties, we would take the ancient wood and wire "sleeping car" from Karachi, across the vast baked-brown plains of Pakistan, through swirling dust storms to Lahore and Peshawar where we'd gain a foothold for the final Jeep dash through the Khyber Pass to the Afghan desert. The courier checked out his sleeping bag and knives and forks, as well as two thermos bottles for water and tea (Old India, you know!). All this from tiny shops in dusty Karachi. Then he would cruise the markets around the town for local "victualers" offering New Zealand and Australian tinned foods which would be the solid chow for the long, lonely trek north to the Afghan capital. Of course, if he were fortunate at certain brief periods of the year, the roadbagger would catch the occasional flight that went to Kabul. The airplane was an old-timer, a U.S. Army Air Corps C-47, unpressurized but converted to civilian use after WWII. The three-hour ride from Karachi to Kabul was tough on smokers because that old bird could not tolerate open flames.

I was on the surface journey to Kabul one fine week in the early 1950s. I had banged and bounced from Karachi across western Pakistan and the Sind Desert on the old train and completed a trainside pouch exchange with our Consulate General folks at Lahore. Quite at home in my vintage compartment which I had bolted against the steady stream of passengers banging on my door, I read, slept, and enjoyed my soups and stews prepared on that old courier ally, the Meta Burner. This was a compact fold-up stove that burned alcohol tablets and was the prized possession of each Paris-based courier in those times of long, transcontinental rail trips. The compartment did not, mercifully, contain a mirror; the passenger, judging from the dust-caked pouches, must have looked like an animated chunk of the Great Indian Desert!

One morning, many moons after boarding this historic and venerable train, I was conveyed in steaming, chugging uncertainty into Peshawar, the fabled key city of the former Northwest Frontier Province of India. Out of the maelstrom of brightly robed, turbaned humanity strode an Afghan chauffeur from our Kabul embassy. His experienced manner was a decided asset as he directed the courier and two pouch-bearing porters through horse-drawn carts and station merchants to the battered green Jeep which would be our wheels through Afghanistan.

A Death at Dean's

First stop after the train was Dean's Hotel, a low, yellowed oasis under the trees, right out of the pages of Kipling's journal. It was here, the Afghan driver told me with mischievous authority, that a Scot officer with the old British Army in India had left his friends at the hotel bar and stepped into the men's toilet. A concealed cobra lashed out at him, bit him severely, and Dean's gained a certain notoriety when the Scot died on the spot.

Breakfast at Dean's that morning for the driver and me, attended tableside by our two big diplomatic pouches, was tea, muffins and porridge, topped off with a real colonial throwback, a warm kippered herring. Thus fortified, we piled into the Jeep and struck out for the long climb from this fertile region to the rocky approaches of the Khyber Pass. This well-worn invasion route to the Indian subcontinent was guarded of course, and the traveler was advised to keep his horse or camel or vehicle moving and not wander off the narrow route. Gun slits manned by sharpshooters dominated the pass from impressive angles and conveyed a sense of clear-cut authority in that craggy terrain.

The Pakistan and Afghanistan border control offices loomed out of the mountain emptiness and passport and customs clearances were short and sweet. The Jeep had to swing from British left side as practiced in Pakistan to drive-right Afghanistan. The hills leveled off as we descended the Khyber's shoulder and dodged the cargo trucks and busses that converged on the frontier. It seemed that soon after entering Afghan territory, the hard road dwindled first into gravel, then dirt and eventually into a few tire tracks here and a couple of camel and donkey trains there. We had about a hundred miles of tough driving ahead of us to Kabul, and the Jeep charged ahead, grinding and whining its way across open desert, up dry riverbeds and through massive rock-strewn plains of primordial beauty. A great cloud of dust on the horizon signaled a large trading caravan of merchant-nomads on their way south to the rich markets of India and Pakistan. We pulled up and peered through the dust at the great, shaggy Bactrian camels swaying their heavy loads of cloth, furs and dates. Ever-present dogs yipped and roamed the route ahead while most of the people in the spectacular train walked beside their beasts. Most of the men and children raised their right hands in the desert salute, but all of the women ignored us in the anonymity of their veiled world. Some hours after we had met the camel train, we found its previous night-camp, a deep hollow at the base of cliffs where animals could be tethered, beds laid, and fires lighted.

Flash Flood!

Subtly from the desolate plain across the oasis of Jalalabad, a patch of fertile green on the quiet, brown earth. It was Nature's breadbasket huddled under the encircling mountains which sent melted snow down to dampen the dry soil and nourish the crops of that barren district. The riverbeds and camel trails formalized into a dirt road as we drew near the oasis which appeared to be a center of excited activity. Horsemen galloped down the road to intercept us and, straddling the route with their mounts, asked if we had medicines. A flash flood had smashed down on the town's north side, citizens had died, animals too, and there was urgent need for medical supplies. A search of the Jeep turned up nothing medical, but I presented them with iodine and a bottle of Halazone water purifiers which I kept in the bottom of my trusty old briefcase. We tried to divert around the town to hit our route north to Kabul but were blocked by collapsed house walls, furniture, mattresses, and other debris that had been flung about by the floodwaters.

After an hour of trying alternate paths past the small community, we encountered an American from the

University of Wyoming; he had learned of our Jeep's arrival and had sought us out to learn the condition of the country to the south which we had just covered. He was an agronomist in a technical assistance U.S.A. program for Afghanistan and had been waiting one day for the flood to recede. He reported that he and his wife and a U.S. marine embassy guard were holed up in a room of the town's inn and that food and water were almost exhausted in the entire community. Even the available water was suspect because of widespread contamination that accompanied the disaster. As one resort they would turn back to Pakistan and after that rough journey find nourishment. But their hope was that the waters would fall, giving them an escape to their Kabul destination. Dead telephones added to the confusion. My cans of New Zealand pork and beans and Australian bully beef zoomed right into the spotlight. We drove directly to the inn where I contributed my entire stock of "Down Under" victuals to the hungry trio. As they consumed the welcome chow, we talked over the big questions: How would we next eat? How long would we hold out in Jalalabad? Would we head north to Kabul or south to Pakistan?

Devastation

The marine, driver, and I jumped into the Jeep with the ever-close pouches and headed out for a quick inspection trip. Again, we found only the route south open. Most of the town and its few exit roads were under water and blocked by floating beds, dead goats, and a sea of impenetrable mud. The grim tally of recovered corpses proceeded on a low hill above the disaster scene. Up to that point some seven citizens had perished in the wall of water that had roared out of the mountains, tearing the community to shreds.

Something threw a flicker of panic into us as we circled the Jeep back to the thin road that led south. Survivors of the tragedy were beginning to trickle out of the broken town; their abandonment of Jalalabad was a signal to us: Get Out! Families hauled their few possessions on their shoulders, in handcarts, or on the backs of scrawny gray donkeys. Food and water lay to the south, and they had forsaken their homes to make the long march to survival. We would soon have to make our decision to stay or follow them. A strategic discovery for us and one that gave us precious time to wait out the flood waters was a mound of watermelons that had avoided the devastation and had suspiciously emerged at precisely the moment of greatest need. The melons brought astronomic prices, a minor concern in view of the liquid and nourishment they provided as eminent disaster food.

Our quintet, fortified with watermelon, holed up in a dingy room at the inn and waited out the dull evening and the very long night. At dawn we sized up the situation: waters were falling, but mud, boulders and timber blocked the thin route north. Dividing our watermelons carefully, we set out on a group inspection, deciding to wait just one-half day longer before wheeling south to safety. As the day came to full light, we saw the ugly hand of flood: crushed and slimed dwellings, drowned animals, and frantic humans tearing at the ruins for lost relatives. Living sounds stilled; people and animals were either dead or filing south on the sole exit route.

Escape!

Our American contingent set up camp at the blocked north exit and tried to select potential paths through the receding water and mud. The Wyoming couple and the marine guard were traveling in a carry-all truck that could power through considerable mud and water so we looked for an opportunity to test it. Now and then we pushed a boulder or an uprooted tree out of the way and poked at mounds of mire to break them down. By now we were down to our last chunks of melon, and the time was at hand for choosing routes north or south. We tried the truck first and it made a short, successful venture into the rock- and mud-fouled water before returning to our jump-off point. I chained our Jeep to the truck, and the two vehicles edged cautiously into the mire at the start of a crawling, suspenseful transit. If we could just keep our momentum, even at 1/4 mile per hour, we could breach the three hundred perilous yards of muck and be on our high road to Kabul. A fragment of optimism can sometimes be an awesome force! The vehicles whined and groaned as they sagged into soft spots but forward we pushed with clay-brown water lapping at the doors.

Twenty agonizing minutes brought us to a rocky creek bed which gave truck and Jeep the traction they needed to gain the roadway on the opposite side. "Damn it," we gasped, "we're on our way!"

We unlinked the Jeep from the truck and roared off to Kabul which was still a long, hungry drive north. But Fate had one more chill for me on that desolate, high mountain road. To keep warm I sat in my sleeping bag which I had pulled up to my neck. This immobilized my arms. Bad decision! As we banged along the rough road in the dark, my door of the Jeep flew open and I slipped halfway out "dressed" in my sleeping bag. I stared into an icy chasm 2000 feet from roadway to canyon below with only my left shoulder blade wedged into enough of the canvas door to hold me. "My Luck, she has saved my Bacon for another day," flashed into my mind about then.

Late that night five humans, just small shadows in the empty Afghan landscape, rolled into the dusty compound of the American embassy. The duty communicator coolly received my two mud-spattered diplomatic pouches, immediately checked for his personal mail and then asked if he might arrange a sandwich for us.

A Pocketful of Amazements

One of the open secrets of historic Frankfurt am Main is that if you tire of the city, you can dive across the River Main and get lost in another world named Sachsenhausen: Saxons Houses. This small enclave embraces food, drink, music, and an atmosphere all its own. Ancient apple-wine houses stand elbow to elbow with jazz cafes. With a right hand a street sausage vendor creates fresh tubes of beef and pork right on the cobblestones while a left hand tends a charcoal fire that keeps the train of food moving. You are never far from a mug of apple-wine (hard cider) or a tankard of world-class pilsner beer. Old drinking songs vie with rock and jazz lyrics in the old wooden bars and inns that bloom every Sachsenhausen night.

It didn't take me long to realize that this 1200-year-old pocket of vitality and medieval lore was my pearl. I toiled in Frankfurt by day and toted my trumpet to Sachsenhausen by night. I ate there, drank there and played my horn there, and I prized my status, after several years' perfect attendance, as a "regular" among the local night people. It struck me as unusually perceptive once when a young lady who had gotten to know my apartment in Frankfurt said suddenly, "I've been trying to determine what it is that makes this place 'feel' like Sachsenhausen . . . it's the apple-wine aroma . . . in your clothes . . . in your trumpet case, everywhere." I had no defense; you could almost touch the apples in the air.

In autumn, horse-drawn wagons full of apples would clip-clop through the old quarter, to be dumped on the ground before the saloons that pressed their own cider. It was a glimpse into medieval history to watch the progress of apples from juice to hard cider through barrel after barrel over many months. The little inns were ageless, incorruptible, and dignified as they dispensed hearty platters of smoked pork chops that had been marinated in sauerkraut juice or a wooden slab bearing fine-chopped raw beef decorated with onions and paprika on dark grain-bread. Of course, standing at attention around these delicious offerings were the golden glasses of apple nectar.

I seemed to gravitate most evenings to the worn, old, comfortable tavern with the impervious name The Brave Nipple. BN was a happy enclave with predictable independence and a history that stretched back to the Middle Ages. Its history was in fact a record of the great European wars that had interrupted the life-sustaining flow of apples from tree to barrel. Other merely mortal antics on the stage of history hardly competed with this mystical fruit on the grand scale of centuries of drinking.

BN was my drop-out pub where I could race through a couple of German and English newspapers, eat something most worthwhile and meet the musicians and other night folk.

I'd like to tell you about the evening a gentleman sat down at BN's long wooden bar and horrified us with his pocketful of tantalizing amazements. He traveled much, said he, spearing my old courier attention in midair. As an incessant traveler he had a very heavy ape that sat squarely on top of his two shoulders. This ape was called Fear of Hotel Fires. My attention span took a light-year leap. Now, he always carried with him this high-tech life-saver. He reached into his pocket and extracted a resilient cord that looked too thin to save anyone's life. It rested neatly in the palm of his hand and ended in a leather grip. Our lecturer flung the cord, and it extended about 409 feet across the barroom floor. The audience had grown somewhat; the master of ceremonies looked around the circle of faces and said he saw disbelief.

"Too small? Too weak? Not at all! This cord will lift a small ox." He looped his line around a steel umbrella stand and lifted his hefty body off the floor.

"With this little buddy, hardly detectable in your pocket, you could lower yourself to safety in many dangerous situations, including strategic escape from the bill collector." Our narrator paused and with great flourish produced what he called this innocent little jewel, a small softgel that could have enormous impact on your interpersonal relationships. It was colorless and reminiscent of a vitamin capsule.

"Let's say you are across the table from the butcher-thug who slashed your sister's face. He has never met you but you have contrived to have a drink with him. The bartender calls the slasher to answer a fake phone call at which moment you drop the end-of-time-bomb into his whiskey-soda. The rendezvous passes and 24 hours later so does the axeman. Technical description of his demise: Chronic Cholesterol-induced Cardiac Arrest which would seem to indicate a rich food and alcohol lifestyle, leading to the terminal heart attack."

Hmm. . . the growing circle of faces murmured its approval. The body press from the back row of this attentive assembly told me that this well-dressed, literate speaker had us in the palm of his hand. separated into halves and out popped one ball bearing and one condom. They had a stunning effect, lying there on the ancient wood of Old Europe. Tricks and Sex! Not a totally dismissable ploy, thought I later, as I trudged over to the Jazz Podium with a golfball and a thin cord parked in my pocket.

Marooned in the Subarctic

I wrapped up a courier tour of duty in Manila, Philippines, and felt great relief at leaving two years of heat and humidity during a period of incessant travel throughout Southeast Asia. As a northerner from the Upper Peninsula of Michigan, I couldn't wait to get home to the cold, pure air of early winter. It was also hunting season, and I planned to head north beyond Lake Superior to the Canadian subarctic to hunt moose before taking up a new assignment in the Middle East. My destination was a cabin on a lake high up in the forested hinterland. Erik and Laura Gran operated a hunt-fish camp there and the only access and exit were by Erik's flight-scarred Cessna airplane which never used wheels. In summer he landed on water pontoons, and in the winter he used plane-skis. Any pilot would love those water-and-snow soft landings. I had just earned my student-pilot rating, and Erik continued my flying education in the spacious northern air.

Sanctuary

The isolation in a winter setting made the tight little camp a virtual sanctuary. Inside the cheery fireplace and hefty meals of roast moose, wild duck with wild rice, partridge and trout. Outside roaring winds and swirling snow under the pines and birches. The main cabin rooms were warmed by the fireplace. The bedrooms were cold. How cold? My personal record was sleeping under furs while the thermometer hanging on the wall stood at minus 38° F.

In the frigid world of ice outside, all living activity seemed to go quiet. Then, why the curious explosions that would crackle at times through the frozen lakes and forest? At this intensely low temperature a tree would expand its liquids to a point at which it would literally explode. I have come upon such exploded trees and have stood in disbelief at the awesome force of deep cold, their trunks were jaggedly ripped apart. For camp chuckles we would soak pancake bits and pieces in whiskey and hang them on bushes where the always-alert jays and crows would attack them. We would laugh with faces pressed against the icy windows as these feathered camp followers began to show the effects of the bourbon booze. They would flop off a bush, flutter out of the snow and take aim on a tree branch but miss it by a mile only to complete the maneuver by making a nice snowdive. Or, one of these flapjack thieves would fly up to a branch, get a grip with unsteady toes, but slide off in a neat somersault. Eventually this funny flying circus tumbled into the snow for a ten-minute hangover before regaining full-flight status. Next morning they were all back at pancake time, and it seems as though they had discussed these amazing exploits with their flocks because the daily swarm of birds increased dramatically.

Fly North!

When skies cleared, Erik and I would unpeel the tarps from the old Cessna and run the engine, quite a feat when the Arctic jet stream would pour minus 40 degree air over the tough little flying machine. We would fly perhaps a hundred miles north and land on a frozen lake where I would take snowshoes, sandwiches, some bourbon, and my rifle for a few hours of hunting. Erik would return in midafternoon to pick me up and fly back to camp. On one of those forays, we saw moose tracks along a low valley. Erik found the white runway of a lake nearby, and I left the airplane for some snowshoe hunting. I worked my way over to the valley in the snow that had been piling up since early autumn, eight feet deep in places. Without those "webs," as the old lumberjacks called snowshoes, a man would be the mortal prisoner of deep snow.

After a few hours of travel in that subarctic stillness, I spotted a lone caribou steaming through a forested hill to the northwest, but no other game. There was a trace of snow in the air as the sky slowly turned green-gray, a sign of imminent snow. I worked my way back to the lake, not wanting to take any chances of missing my pick-up by Erik. By early afternoon the wilds had taken on that etched black look that will not absorb light. It was much darker than the usual dusk. With this deepening tone came the wind and the promised snow. Suddenly I realized that there could not be an airplane that day. Erik was probably pinned down at his camp: I had before me a night in the icy jungle of the north.

No Return

I holed up on the lee side of the lake, dragging fallen branches together for firewood and breaking off heavy spruce boughs for a makeshift shelter. Curls of birch bark ignited quickly to get my fire blazing, just in time, since the snow came driving at sharp angles from a dark sky. Making my wilderness camp kept me on the jump, and when at last I sat down and looked at my watch, I got a shock: it was only four-fifteen. The storm had brought on early darkness, and a long night loomed ahead of me. My equipment stood at a rifle with a dozen Cal. 30-06 cartridges, two sandwiches, a half-pint of bourbon, some one-a-day vitamins, tough hunting clothes, and a pair of absolutely essential snowshoes. But I needed two more things: (1) a weather report and (2) a telephone. I could forget about them in this huge, empty sweep of forest and frozen lakes that had rarely felt a human foot since the Ice Age.

As my fire consumed lengths of wood, I pulled in the unburnt ends to keep a continuous flame; my watch seemed stalled. It was only five o'clock. I tried dozing. After some time I stole a glance at my watch: 5:35. This was going to be some standoff between time, the storm and me. I saved my sandwiches and a tip of bourbon with snow chaser. Then I fell asleep plotting my activities for the return of light at dawn.

Crack! A loud noise snapped me out of my snooze just as I felt my entire camp fall about three feet from its former perch on the ice shelf to a dry leaf scattered forest floor. I scrambled to retrieve valuable pieces of my burning wood and was astonished to be gazing into a mid-autumn scene where moments before it had been Arctic winter. The fire had cracked the shelf ice and dumped me and my camp on the floor of the great northern forest. My new site made wood gathering easier, and I rearranged my spruce boughs into a bed of sorts. But time would not budge. I tried ignoring my watch and ran through plans for the morning. Several times I floated the idea of trying to slosh my way out of the north woods, but showshoeing a hundred miles across that wilderness, given my meager supplies, canceled that notion. I had to wait out the storm at this known location.

White Night

Dozing and sleep flickered on and off as the heavens raged above me. My appetite behaved admirably, deciding to tune out until I had figured where I would find my future meals. The sandwiches and vitamin tablets would be saved to the last. What if the blizzard went on for days? No airplane could fly; yes, the vitamins would be decisive. I had always told myself that if I were taken prisoner by terrorists in some dangerous corner of the world, I would strengthen my mind by reviewing Latin and German grammar or by mentally writing stories. The tales would be of my adventures as a Ten Million Mile Diplomatic Courier. Holed up and isolated under the Big North blizzard, I found that mental exercises and story writing were hard to find. The reality of my predicament dominated from stage center.

Peeking at my watch I found that I had reached eleven o'clock. Only nine hours to daybreak! The temperature as we flew out of camp had been minus 15° F. It had to be minus 20° or lower now but my fire and solid clothes kept me warm.

Midnight, one-twenty, three, four-thirty. When I

finally stood up and stuck my head out into the white gale, a greenish pallor of snow carried a hint of daylight. It was time to execute Plan 1: I would hike out to the middle of the frozen lake and march off a huge BOB as a snow signature for any pilot in the region. However, thick snow obliterated my tracks in minutes, forcing me back to my ice cave to wait out this downfall. Midmorning brought a sharp drown in the wind, and I celebrated that event by wolfing down a half sandwich. An hour later the snowfall thinned, and I went to work tracking out the B-O-B with my snowshoes. By now my ears were playing tricks on me, and I thought I "heard" airplane after airplane boring holes through the howling cold above me. By noon it was my opinion that I now had flying weather despite light snow flurries. I stood in my hole at the edge of the ice shelf where my fire sent a good signal of blue smoke. My B-O-B remained visible on the lake ice while I tired of processing false alarms of airplanes from my ears. My eyes were riveted to the south. Was that tiny speck on the horizon a hawk or an airplane? I tracked it with great intensity . . . before I could decide what it was, I heard the familiar whir of Erik's Cessna. Whew! He made it!

The Most Beautiful Bird in the World

I scrambled to the lake center and waved a snowshoe in wide circles. Erik's grinning face was pressed against the cockpit window as he made a slow inspection pass. Lining up against the breeze, he let his beautiful little bird set down on its skis. When I reached the plane he shouted "What did you do, sleep in your fire? You're black with soot." I buried my fire in the snow and quickly loaded my gear for the escape flight. But, oh no, we were not going to get away that easy. Wet snow clung to the plane skis and we could not ski the little craft into flight. First, we tracked down a snowshoe runway. Then we lifted each ski and ran a hunting knife along it to remove ice and snow. We piled into the willing little kite and made a furious run down our manmade airstrip. No go! We could not force the plane into the air. We halted and stripped the bird of rifles, an axe, one seat, a chain, a coil of rope, and one pair of our precious two sets of snowshoes. After scraping the skis again we roared off across the clinging ice. After an eternity the skis bounced up and hung half an inch above the lake for almost a full minute before Erik pulled the nose up and headed for camp. My eyes locked onto the still, desolate scene of my Arctic outpost. Our jettisoned equipment lay next to our snowshoed runway. Erik would retrieve everything the next day. My thoughts darted at once to camp. Ah, fireplace and a hot meal!

Polar Pioneer Nobile Alive in Rome!

In 1926 the world was startled to learn that an Italian airship pilot, Umberto Nobile, had flown across the North Pole with a group of distinguished explorers. In addition to its daring first transit of the pole, the flight created high anxiety in international capitals because radio contact with the expedition was lost shortly after the airship *Norge* swung north from its mooring mast in Spitsbergen. The *Norge* navigated through sleet and ferocious winds to reach its polar goal and then continued across the top of the earth, revealing to Nobile and his companions man's first view of unknown expanses around the world dome. The passengers were no less than Roald Amundsen, Norwegian conqueror of the South Pole, and his countryman Hjalmar Riiser-Larsen, along with American Lincoln Ellsworth. After a long and tense silence a weak radio signal crackled from Teller, Alaska: "*Norge* crash-landed at Teller. All safe."

This drama from the classic age of polar exploration was much on my mind as I traveled through the Spitsbergen isles. I made my way to Ny-Ålesund, perhaps the world's most northerly community, and stood in midsummer snow at the mooring mast used half a century earlier by Nobile to anchor his great airship. In the purity of the Arctic air, *Norge*'s mast still stood in silent tribute to these brave flyers.

The Italia

In 1928 Nobile, who was an airship designer and navigator who flew his own craft, led another polar expedition north in the newly constructed *Italia.* He again crossed the North Pole but the *Italia* was gripped in a massive Arctic storm that drove it down to the ice pack. The cockpit-gondola smashed on the surface and the huge body of the airship tore loose and floated away in the raging storm with eleven crew members trapped inside. They were never seen again. Nobile and seven of his companions were eventually rescued after agonizing months on the ice pack but the catastrophe took 17 lives, including that of Roald Amundsen whose airplane was lost at sea in the search for the stricken *Italia.*

Standing in Spitsbergen at the very take-off point of the *Norge* and the *Italia* made a lasting impression on me. I wondered if I might find in Italy some relics of the expeditions. A map, a compass, pictures? My diplomatic courier routes took me to Rome some time later, and I combed the museums of air history and exploration. Not a mention of the Nobile flights or of the *Norge* and *Italia.* As I awaited my next courier run to our Rome embassy, I was advised to forget the Nobile flights which were linked to great human loss and were therefore unsuitable for museum sponsorship. That evaluation struck me as bizarre until I recalled the glory-oriented Fascisti who rose to power in Italy under Benito Mussolini precisely during the era of Nobile's polar flights. With their total state of control, the Fascisti consigned the airship crash to historical oblivion. Yes, that had to explain my failure to locate anything from the *Norge* and *Italia* flights.

On yet another trip to our Rome embassy my chauffeur discussed these matters with me and made an articulate suggestion, "Why don't you telephone some of the Nobiles in the city directory? See if someone is related to Umberto Nobile."

I flew to the Rome telephone directory, and my eyes locked instantly onto Prof-Gen U. Nobile. "The name and ranks of this great explorer live yet in this old world," said I. The embassy telephone operator called the listed number: no answer. She jotted down the street address for me, and I waded into Via Veneto in search of a taxi. What did I think I would learn by probing ancient Rome with my dreams of a grand expedition half a century ago? Perhaps I would locate a relative or even a neighbor of the historic dirigible captain Nobile. Someone might point me in the right direction to a small provincial museum that held a photo, a stained navigation chart, a faded flag. . . . There must be some remnant of this world-class explorer.

The Quest

The taximan dropped me at the scribbled address. Here was a Rome I had not yet seen: wide avenues, expanses of lawn, rich shrubbery, very old palm trees. The house number was visible but an entrance was not in view. One had to walk around the structure to reach the entrance. It was clear that this was a comfortable, well-situated town villa. A single, well-polished plate read: Professore-Generale U. Nobile. There was neither bell nor buzzer, so I tried the door handle: locked. Standing back I surveyed the entrance and the upper floors of the building. Totally lost in this exercise, I was startled to hear a voice behind me: "Nobile?"

I wheeled around to face a young man who had interrupted my daydreaming. I replied, "Si, Nobile."

He strode past me and selected an ornate key from a noisy collection that hung from his belt. The door opened and as I entered he pointed skyward and said: "*Sommittà*" (Top).

I replied: "*Grazie*" (Thanks). Somewhat bewildered, I stepped into a luxurious elevator, pressed the *sommittà* button and was conveyed upward to an experience that will remain with me for the rest of my life.

As I emerged from the elevator I found myself before a massive oaken door which bore yet another brass plate reading: Professore-Generale U. Nobile.

Polar Pioneer Nobile Alive?

A long shining metallic rod arched down from the ceiling and ended in a ceramic handle. I pulled on it and heard a deep, rich bell tone that conveyed to me a sense of timelessness. It told me for example that one ring of this bell would suffice . . . I would not even think of ringing again. Many minutes passed. I stood, suspended in time and thought, before that great door. There was complete, enveloping silence. Then, without the slightest noise, the door moved! It inched inward. A figure limped to the doorway . . . a very old man with long rolls of paper under one arm. I greeted him with: *"Buon giorno"* (Good day), offering him my personal calling card. He motioned me inside and quietly led me through a beautiful hall which was lined with old photographs and period furniture. The photographs had an electrifying impact on me even as we moved slowly to the sitting room. I could not believe my senses; was it possible that Umberto Nobile himself was limping a few feet ahead of me?

We seated ourselves at the corner of a low table, and I looked into the eyes of Umberto Nobile, alive at 90 years of age! So efficiently had the Fascisti consigned him to oblivion that his existence had interest only for scholars and the rare historian.

An Italian Navy petty officer arose from a typewriter in an adjoining room and proceeded without comment to pour two robust Fundador brandies. Nobile addressed me in English: "You are in the Diplomatic Service? Not from the publishers?" No, I was a student of the classic age of polar air exploration . . . I had recently been to the *Norge* and *Italia* mooring mast in Spitsbergen. I halted at that point. As the words rolled from my mouth, this ancient navigator placed his left arm on my hand and stared for several long minutes. "Spitsbergen" escaped from his lips. Then silence.

Such was the unreal atmosphere of my pilgrimage that led me to a living legend of the Arctic. When I protested at the total absence of museum recognition of his polar flights, he led me to a large wing of his villa. Here was the museum I sought: maps, dirigible blueprints, torn canvas, compasses, sextants, propeller blades, flying uniforms. Nobile's pet dog that survived the *Italia* crash had been mounted and added to the museum. The walls and tables were heavy with photographs and books. Logbooks from the *Italia* and *Norge* lay atop lecterns. Roald Amundsen, Lincoln Ellsworth, and Umberto Nobile echoed from the exhibits and from the walls. My amazing host pointed to a picture of the *Italia* crash site showing him lying on the ice near a tent. He said that his leg was so badly smashed that even after the rescue he never regained its full use. That was evident here, fifty years after those tragic events, as he hobbled past the tools and the memories of his grand expeditions. He was completing a book on the *Italia* crash; its title was *The Red Tent,* taken from the tattered emergency tent carried by the airship. It was dug out of the crash debris and gave the few survivors their only protection from the raging weather of the ice cap. The Italian Navy sent him the petty officer to help organize the writing of the book which would later become a feature film starring Sean Connery and Claudia Cardinale. Revenues from the book and film would go to the aid of the survivors of the men who lost their lives in the tragedy. This crippled old commander was standing by his men to the last.

We returned to his sitting room, and despite his age he showed a bright mentality as he reviewed his long career in airship exploration. I was greatly interested in his description of the *Norge* transit of the North Pole in 1926. Nobile was the designer and pilot of the craft but Amundsen was the commander of this Norwegian expedition. As the great ship neared 90 degrees North, the pole, Amundsen ordered total radio silence that was actually observed, reported Nobile, until *Norge* crash-landed in Alaska. This break in communication, coming at the most critical point of their dangerous flight, created an international wave of anxiety that exploded in relief and joy when the crew radioed its victorious message.

Several hours later as I walked slowly through this historic city, I could not believe I had, with incredible luck, discovered Umberto Nobile alive in modern Rome. He had invited me to visit him again, and I made three more calls at his villa where I met his German wife and several relatives of his lost crewmen. He inscribed a copy of his book to me, and, in one of two letters he sent me, he enclosed a signed picture taken during the triumphant cross-country tour of the United States following the *Norge* flight. Professor-General Umberto Nobile worked on his lost crewmen until his death in 1978 at age 93 years.

Barroom Theater

Hanging at the bottom of Africa, Cape Town has it geographic allure and a feisty waterfront to distinguish it from a dozen other oceanic ports of call. Freighters from India, oil tankers from Kuwait, and scientific ships from Antarctica pause at this strategic harbor. So do diplomatic couriers who reach the end of the continent and the turnaround airline routes.

Our courier hotel was perched smack in the middle of the bustling docks area, and you got the impression that as soon as you had registered at the desk and dropped your luggage, you could stride right out into this surging sea of humans and maritime atmosphere. The city fathers had reclaimed ancient warehouses and converted them to bars, shops, and restaurants. Quickly I discovered a musty old freight office that had been magically transformed into a brewery! The brewer himself was the boss, and he ordered me to drink only his best product, a dark, tough ale bearing the name Bosun's Bitter. I mentioned Bosun's Bitter specifically because a good crock of it was literally snatched from my hand and demolished in a hilarious incident that first night in Cape Town.

Big Brawl

It all started when I heard some very good piano notes wafting through the salty air of the dock world. There are two things I cannot ignore: a cute girl and the sound of live music. The last of these two pulled me into view of the first. I tracked the piano notes to a low, angled jazz spot that was built of massive logs that gave the joint some exceptional acoustics. Just as I hit the doorway, a tenor sax, bass, and drums hit a nice jazz chord with the piano, and suddenly we had a quartet live on the Cape Town waterfront. A marvelously constructed Portuguese chick brought the mike to her lips and recreated the jazz anthem "Round Midnight," and I leaned into my mug of Bosun's Bitter. Nice setting. Good music. That rare balance of forces lasted about two minutes when I saw the singer's eyes widen and heard her voice quaver. . . .

I turned to see what had distracted her just as two giant Dutchmen, one shirtless, crashed along a line of tables, fighting, cursing, and wrestling through, upon and over customers, waitresses, and one U.S. diplomatic courier. Their language of battle was Afrikaans, a Dutch-derived tongue that in itself sounds like feeding time in the lions' den. The noise rose to a howl as the fight engulfed the bandstand. Remembering the *Titanic,* some of the musicians tried to play on, but that noble try was wiped out when one of the combatants was thrown right on top of the piano. I think I heard a surrealist chord bonk out of the keyboard as this shirtless warrior arose and flung his attacker against the bandstand wall, pinning a very surprised saxophonist and pianoman under him. Things were clicking by so fast that I hadn't chosen sides in the melee.

Fate Steals a Skirt

Now, four blue-clad Keystone Cops with white helmets and red billy clubs entered from stage left just as our Portuguese songstress's flowing skirt was pinned against the bass drum by a falling music stand. She whirled to free herself and to dodge the charge of the cops, but grinning Fate stole away her skirt and revealed two sculpted legs that almost terminated the brawl right there. No matter; the battle resumed but not for long because someone had summoned the boss of the joint, a monster who silenced the gladiators and brought order to the quartet of peace officers who looked as if they were conducting a Shanghai fire drill. Suddenly, music again filled the air but the quartet had become a trio since the saxman and his horn had been partially wrecked in the disturbance. I found a new Bosun's Bitter to replace the mug that had been demolished in the first wave of battle and sat back to look over the quieting pub. Peering through the haze, I made out the name of this little jewel: Club-Jazz Theater. In years of nosing around the exotic Cape Town waterfront, I could not escape the thought that this elaborate explosion might have been just a bit of midnight theater.

Treasure of the Nile

As a rookie courier working in and out of Cairo I took a great liking to my "hotel." It was a venerable Nile River steamer, the *Arabia,* that had been tied up at a convenient, appealing spot on the riverbank. It was an easy stroll to the grand Museum of Egyptian Antiquities, and it was the ideal home base for the traveling courier.

The diverse clientele of the Arabia would convene on the afterdeck for evening cocktails and leisurely conversation. Gin seemed to be in every glass in myriad combinations. Scotch and bourbon were in scarce supply and the Egyptian beer was underwhelming. On occasion some of us would get into a crap game before dinner was served, and the Egyptian pounds, British pounds and American dollars flew almost as fast as the dice.

I was astride one of these crap games one Cairo evening with another courier, a British businessman, a Dane and two Egyptians. The wagering was fast and furious, and we ignored the dinner announcement in pursuit of the dice. One of the Egyptians bowed out of the contest but informed us that he would return shortly. When he strode onto the afterdeck half an hour later, he held a rolled carpet in his hands. He stated that since it was not possible to raise cash for our game, he would like to gamble against the value of the high-quality Persian carpet he offered. The British gentleman and the Egyptian gentleman examined the carpet and advised the rest of us non-experts that it was indeed a splendid creation. We agreed on its gaming value, about $700, and the dice resumed their vicious cycles. Near midnight, hunger and the exhaustion of most players' funds brought the Arabia Dice Marathon to a halt. The Dane and the carpet-bearing Egyptian were broke and I, the new kid on deck, held the prized carpet. We telephoned two taxis and off we went for a superb late meal at the edge of the desert in the vicinity of the ancient Pyramids and Sphinx of Giza. It was an exotic setting, and a couple of us winners footed the bill for our losers.

I carried my beautiful carpet from assignment to assignment. It lay on polished floors in Paris, Manila, Frankfurt, Panama, Athens and Bangkok. Then, I committed an error. I "loaned" it to my girlfriend who was refurbishing her apartment. Her marvelous cat, in just ten days, reduced my Persian wonder to a layer of colorful dust. What an end for my Treasure of the Nile.

Where's Grandma?

An old shiny Buick station wagon rumbled down the Mexican coastal road headed for Guadalajara. The passengers were two parents, two sons, and grandmother who was ailing but carefully wrapped in a blanket with a wool shawl over her head. Atop the station wagon was a long luggage rack that carried cooped chickens, suitcases, and several young palm trees with ear balls wrapped around their roots. Cruising down the coast under the brilliant sun, the vehicle was a stirring sight with palm trees swaying above the cages of shrieking chickens.

In that remote region travelers wisely carried food and drink, and when Mama signed a pleasant little green valley a few hundred yards off the roadway, our tight family decided to halt and have a rest and a picnic at the same time. The boys bounded off like mountain ponies while their parents dug out food and utensils for the fresh-air meal. Grandma announced that she would have a cup of bottled water and would remain in the station wagon. She did not feel up to maneuvering through the rocky terrain to the picnic site even if it were a grassy plot. When Father and Mother had prepared the meal, they called the boys, and the quartet thoroughly enjoyed its open-air lunch. Mama asked Papa to take a slice of fruit back to the car for Grandma. She and the boys continued eating, and Papa climbed up the roadside to make a shocking discovery.

Grandma had fallen halfway out of the station wagon rear door. He raced to her side and knew at once that she had passed away! He tried to revive his mother-in-law but there was not a sign of life. Then, the enormity of this tragedy hit him. What would he say to his wife, and to the boys? He set a plan of action. First, he wrapped Grandma's body in her blanket and placed it atop the station wagon, securing it firmly with rope. He straightened up the bottles, newspapers and other contents of the vehicle. From the leather side pocket of his door, he pulled out a flask of tequila, took a swig, and braced himself for the return of his family. How would he be able to tell his wife that her dear mother had just died? And the boys? How could he soften the shock to them?

When he approached the cheerful picnic site, he could not at first bring himself to speak. He sat quietly at his wife's side. When the boys ran off to play, Papa took Mama's hands. Sadness descended over his face like a black fog. "Grandma has just died," he sobbed.

His wife jumped to her feet defiantly. "No. . . she cannot die, not here, not now. . .," she cried. The stricken wife and mother ran toward the roadway, falling and sliding as she went. Papa gathered up the picnic relics and started up the incline. Above him he saw his wife standing on the road, shouting and waving her hands. He hurried along and at last could heard her voice: "Where have you put her? Where is our car?"

Papa could not believe the scene that met his eyes. His wife was standing on an empty roadside. The station wagon had vanished! Not another vehicle was in sight. The two hapless humans looked at each other and in one voice screamed, "Bandidos!" That scourge of the desolate road, the dreaded highwaymen, had struck. Now their calamity had assumed catastrophic dimensions; they had suffered the death of dearly loved Grandma whose body was now racing through the mountains atop a Buick station wagon that was this little family's most valuable asset.

Numbed, the parents were standing motionless in each other's arms when their running youngsters popped over the road's edge. Their voices echoed down the valley: "Where's Grandma?"

Echoes From The Real World

Seen and heard on all trips around the world —

His cabin was close enough to be far enough away . . . and far enough away to be close enough.

When he was young he longed to grow to be an old man . . . at 24 he was.

The wild weather was the proud weather of the high Indians; the weak weather was the choice weather of the low Indians.

Watch, review your memory and choose . . . to prosper.

Life is as inspiring and beautiful as our physical and mental condition permits it to be.

She ran through his money like a pyromoneyac.

Their man in Chicago was as slippery as a lemon seed.

After the war she attended a victory soiree in Paris. For a gown she stripped a velvet drape from her window and became the belle of the ball.

———— • ————

A minute is only a trifle of time . . . unless there's a horse standing on your foot.

———— • ————

These couriers do not race round the earth chasing the sun; they lead it.

———— • ————

She went from teenager to housewife in one weekend.

———— • ————

He thought he was the prince but he could never produce his crown.

———— • ————

After duty in 197 foreign lands, it's clear that human similarities far outclass their differences.

———— • ————

He honored freedom of religion and practiced freedom from religion.

———— • ————

The IQ of the owner is inversely proportional to the length of his car.

———— • ————

When they changed the color of diplomatic pouches to tangerine, was it an affinity for prison-orange or a Freudian slip?

———— • ————

If they left an inch or two in their mugs, it was labeled alcohol abuse.

———— • ————

A minor error in the High Arctic can mean instant death.

———— • ————

Wearing all his medals, he clanked around like a Mexican general.

———— • ————

Draped in her jewelry, she clanked around like a Russian general.

———— • ————

The well-seasoned Norse fisherman mused: "Yaah, we fish and make love in the summer, 'course we can't fish in the winter."

———— • ————

Everyone loved the silent film goddess Peal White. Said the lumberjack: "I'd cut fifteen logs underwater just to sleep with her socks."

———— • ————

Gore Lumbago's music is better than it sounds.

———— • ————

Inflation has arrived on the golf course when you get hit by two golf balls and someone shouts "Eight!"

———— • ————

The czar of auto-vision tests himself couldn't see a Rhino in a clothes closet.

———— • ————

"I sensed immediately that here was an exceptional man," said a Boer War prisoner of war, describing a fellow escapee with whom he hid under an animal shed during a South African thunderstorm. That "exceptional man" turned out to be Winston Churchill, future world statesman.

———— • ————

The old timber cruiser worked alongside his employees in the North Country. When he passed on, a woodsman paid him this tribute: "Old Ed made sure he paid his help before their sweat was dry."

———— • ————

It was a late-night jam session at the rear of a Chicago jazz club. Sitting just offstage was an old-timer listening closely to the players, his hat tipped forward over his eyes. Eventually he leaned over and pulled a glistening trumpet from a battered paper bag, mounted the podium, and blew all the hornmen out the alley door.

———— • ————

He did everything in isolation, yet never felt lonely.

———— • ————

We met on a tropical beach of an Indian Ocean island. She wore an alluring bikini. At dinner that evening with friends she was a very pretty young lady in a party dress. Then, she dropped her bombshell. Said she, "Bob has never seen me with my clothes on. . . ."

———— • ————

Harry's driest Martini was perfected by permitting a

light beam to pass through a closed jug of vermouth onto the gin and cracked ice.

———— • ————

The courier arcs our planet; he is the sun-pacer.

———— • ————

In all the massive tide of this world's history, you are the only you who has ever existed and you stand now on the threshold of the only minute this planet has ever seen.

———— • ————

Our pitcher was the legendary Ace Loone, a guy who could blaze a T-bone steak past a starving grizzly.

———— • ————

At a White House banquet honoring U.S. Nobel Prize medalists, John F. Kennedy noted, "Never has this room seen such an assembly of brilliance since Thomas Jefferson dined here, alone."

———— • ————

Fishing is not a matter of life and death . . . it's more important than that.

———— • ————

The bar's Happy Hour is always preceded by the Attitude Adjustment Hour.

———— • ————

She boarded a long-range bus in Australia and asked for his seat because, she announced, she was "preggers." Standing, he casually asked how long she had been pregnant. Her reply: "About a half hour, mate, and am I tired."

If you can't improve on silence, keep your mouth shut.

———— • ————

Everything has an end, except the sausage which has two.

———— • ————

On a beauty scale of one to ten, she came in at fifteen.

———— • ————

When he sought special attention at a lavish hotel, he and a briefcase-toting aide would stroll through the executive offices like the new owners, traveling incognito.

———— • ————

Your theory is just outrageous enough to be absolutely right.

———— • ————

We pile up our problems ten-by-ten, but we have to solve them one-by-one.

———— • ————

At age 20 he believed in long engagements; at age 38 he could not stand long introductions.

———— • ————

He knew the exact price of everything but never understood the value of anything.

———— • ————

Forget the waves—measure the tides.

———— • ————

Forsake the bronze and granite . . . the imperishable monument is the living tree.

———— • ————

The Mozee-kwaffle of the Contra-Gyrosscopic Relavatator is equal to the Soyafactor of the Ding-how-Rami.

———— • ————

Old Seaman: You're not gonna hang if you were meant to drown.

———— • ————

Road directions to desolate Alpine hamlet: I know it's on the map, but you can't get there from here.

———— • ————

Of a heroic football player: His team didn't win the game, but he did.

———— • ————

Words are not adequate, that's why we have music.

———— • ————

His horn played in thirty foreign languages.

———— • ————

Half an hour's trumpet blowing equals the therapy of a mile's run.

———— • ————

Their reach exceeded their grasp.

———— • ————

I am a benign sinner, but a devout one. The International Date Line converges precisely with the South Pole.

———— • ————

Seated at the South Pole were a Protestant scientist and a Catholic priest. As they were about to devour a beef sandwich, the Padre exclaimed: "Oh, I can't eat this; it's Friday!" The scientist quickly reassured him: "Here, Father, let me trade seats with you. . . . It's still Thursday over here."

———— • ————

The Cornhuskers' helmets bear a big N that stands for Knowledge.

———— • ————

Anatomy tells us that the right side of the brain controls the left side functions of the body, and the left side of the brain controls the right side functions. This means that only left-handed people are in their right brain.

———— • ————

It takes food on the table to make the plates shine.

———— • ————

Sprawled out in his easy chair, he looked like a dozing hunk of fatigue; we learned quickly that he was actually rehearsing for action.

———— • ————

She has the mind of a savant and the heart of a kid.

———— • ————

A limerick in Nepal:

Behold the splendiferous yak,
From the Himalaya far off the track,
His wool in truth is a bit uncouth,
But it does keep the flak off your back.

———— • ————

The salty old divorce lawyer mused: Why spoil such a beautiful relationship by getting married?

———— • ————

We were so scrutinized and evaluated that one day we had become certified squares with documents to prove it.

———— • ————

Their idea of radical chic was to subscribe to a controversial magazine.

———— • ————

One look at the railroad station and you knew this country was neck-deep in the tenth century.

———— • ————

The Anti-Tighten-Up Motto:

> When you smolder and your duds look baggier,
> Why grow older and daily crabbier?
> Grab a relax or break out the juice,
> But whatever you do, don't drop your loose.

———— • ————

Looks like the world confirms that there's no aphrodisiac like a new girlfriend.

———— • ————

The barman informed us: "I'm the boss, but I don't touch the stuff myself, unless I'm alone or with someone." He was the gentleman who said, "You can lead a horticulture but you cannot make her think."

———— • ————

Television has brought to mankind the most precious democratic invention of this fading century: the mute button.

Madame Otro wryly observed: "The Otro diamond is like the Hope diamond in that it comes with a curse, Senator Otro."

———— • ————

You know what Greek god Zeus said to mirror-struck Narcissus: Good-bye and watch yourself."

———— • ————

If the weather forecast is for a 20% chance of rain, do I buy 80% of a raincoat?

———— • ————

Soon after the forecast of a cloudy overcast I had to shovel two inches of overcast off my porch.

———— • ————

The snap judgement is followed by the biting remark.

———— • ————

Colder than an Eskimo knuckle.

———— • ————

Colder than a Siberian outhouse.

———— • ————

Mix objectivity and super-awareness in the crucible of Art and wait: Genius could flash for an instant.

———— • ————

Foreman says to ace riveter, "Listen, Riley, Mrs. Clark across the street complained that she heard some bad language from you today."

Riley responds, "Yeah, Chief, when Mike was tossing those red-hot rivets to me up on the rig, one of 'em rolled down my pant leg and whacked me in the Crown

Jewels. It was at that time that I cautioned him to be more careful with his rivet-tossing."

———— • ————

He was excessively health-conscious; for example, he checked himself into intensive care to cure his dirty fingernails.

———— • ————

A clothing store on a popular beach in Australia does a brisk business selling slightly defective items labeled "Elegant Errors."